The
HERALDING

Ashley
McCarthy

The Heralding

ISBN: Print edition – 978-1-8384121-0-4
        Digital edition – 978-1-8384121-1-1

Typesetting and Production: Catherine Williams, Chapter One Book Production
Cover Design: Michelle Fairbanks, Fresh Design
Proofreading: Craig Smith, CRS Editorial

Printed in the United Kingdom

DEDICATION

Myer, for making me brave

CHAPTER 1

April 1316

The sky did not weep that morning.

A grey curtain enveloped the sodden landscape, behind which the sun fought to cast its warmth. The cowslips lay sad, battling to flower. Yellow should signal spring and regrowth; the feeling that the year will be brighter. In past years, they were as bright as the sun, screaming to be noticed as they lined well-worn paths as if to accompany travellers on their journeys. They would offer happy homes to joyful bees. But this year the rain hammered at any petals that had the temerity to challenge it and they drooped and wilted before succumbing to rot with a sigh. A lonely bee could sometimes be seen searching for the flowers' opening to no avail.

The early frost had begun to fade as Matilda peered outdoors. She opened the door wider and leaned forward to grab some rosemary. A lone sprig would suffice for remembrance.

Closing the door did little to battle the cold and damp.

Nothing had been truly dry for weeks and Galeran lay rigid in his winding sheet, waiting patiently. Maerwynn, a family friend and well known to the villagers, had helped lay him out and now sat on the chair at his side, watching Matilda with sympathy.

Matilda nodded. The candles had gone out but there was no need to relight them now. There were no more prayers left to say. They would make no difference, anyway. Silently, she sank to sit at Maerwynn's feet. There was nought to do but wait. Maerwynn sang softly and stroked Matilda's hair. Matilda sighed and stared into nothingness.

The rancid stench of death lingered in the house.

Nearly an hour passed before a rap on the door broke Maerwynn's song, demanding their attention. It opened immediately and Roger poked his head through the gap. 'I have him,' he said. 'He was in his cups but I didn't let him refuse.'

He paused as Matilda got to her feet. 'I am indebted to you,' she said.

Matilda believed herself blessed to have Roger as her neighbour. Although he worked the land from dawn to dusk, he still found time to offer aid whenever he saw a need – usually before anyone asked. His weathered face was lined with forty summers or more of laughter and kindness, but now his eyes were filled with sorrow. It was his loss, too; Galeran was as a son to him.

'I'll take him to the church,' said Roger. 'While the priest is readying himself, I'll go fetch Howard – he can help me carry Galeran.'

'I shall be heavily indebted.'

'And there will be a time for you to repay your debt – but not today.'

She would repay her debt – if she lived long enough. When the rains began last spring, they'd all grumbled good-heartedly, relieved that the late hard frosts and their accompanying flurries of sleet and hailstones had ceased. Last year's piercing winds had brought in their wake a hot dry summer that baked the chalk ground bone-hard. They were still ploughing in October, struggling to save what they could of the meagre harvest. People went hungry to feed their oxen and horses, and to pay for new ploughboards and buy ale for the ploughmen. But there had been bad harvests before. They'd manage somehow.

The grain couldn't ripen and good bread had become scarce. A luxury. Prices had been high before but the villagers hadn't known they were blessed. Scarcity drove the costs of even the most basic things to a level beyond the means of many. From spring to midsummer, prices had risen until they'd doubled or more. The King's orders to hold prices down had no power when hungry traders refused to listen.

No one had expected the rain to fall for so long when it finally arrived that autumn.

Matilda dreaded ever having to go to market again. Following the long path that avoided the steep climb of Giant's Grave Hill, it rose and dipped as if by a whim. All looked so much bleaker from higher ground. The downs looked grey and brown – not green as they should have;

The mention of Galeran's name stung Matilda. She opened her mouth as if to object but Roger held up his hand. 'A cart won't move through the mud. Thom is a fine horse but he needs to be fresh for working later. We can't risk tiring him.'

'It'll not tire him to go such a short distance,' Matilda said peevishly.

'But it will tire him to work for all who ask the lend of him. And today it will be hard to say no. I'll return shortly.'

Matilda opened her mouth to argue but swiftly closed it, realising Roger was right. She wasn't in a fit mind to say no to anyone. And they would ask. Someone would ask There was always work a horse would make easier, but i would be up to Matilda to find the extra feed Thom woul need, and there was little enough as it was.

Roger retreated and closed the door gently.

'Sit,' said Maerwynn. 'Save your strength.'

Matilda nodded and returned to sit at Maerwynn feet. 'I thought we'd have to bury him without churc she said.

'There's always a priest to be bought,' Maerwynn s in a matter-of-fact tone. 'He'll be rubbing his hands n contemplating the profit he will make today.'

Matilda's eyes widened. She hadn't though payment.

As if reading her mind, Maerwynn contin 'That is not for you to fret about. Roger will mak arrangement.'

3

the colours had been washed away by the rain and only the harsh and tangled gorse seemed to survive. The trees in the forest drooped, bringing her heart down. Instead of feeling the bounce of new life beneath her steps, she had to drag her feet through mud and flint. And she watched her feet not simply to save herself from a fall, but also because the longer she looked across the downs, the sadder the land seemed to grow.

Even the costs of pots and urns had risen as everyone sought to dry what they could indoors. And salt – they fought over what they bought from passing pedlars. There was hardly enough to preserve all the meat. Roger had told Matilda that he'd seen beasts left to litter the fields when he walked with the sheep. His flock was small compared to many – some owned hundreds of sheep. Usually, the dry higher land kept them safe from foot rot, but not anymore. They cast their beady eyes on passers-by as if to let them know that they owned the land. But all the flocks were fast shrinking. And more and more were being claimed by the rivers that surrounded their lands. With rising waters sheep would tumble in when they sought a drink, weighed down by their heavy coats to their fast-flowing death. Things hadn't got so bad in their village – yet. But when people passed through, the villagers measured them according to the size of their bellies and thanked God when they moved on.

And as if hunger weren't enough, as if the constant growl of their bellies and the cries of children tugging at their heartstrings was somehow insufficient, pestilence had followed close behind. Maerwynn had wept when she delivered the first dead child. By the fifth she was thanking God for taking it early.

Galeran had succumbed to the pestilence. Others had, too. A few left fearfully under cover of night, taking what money and valuables they could to pay their way, but there was nowhere to run from this. Father Luke had been one such. He'd emptied the church's coffers and disappeared three weeks ago. No one knew where. No one now cared.

Maerwynn stood and poured two cups of ale, handing one to Matilda. 'Drink,' she said. 'Roger will soon return.'

Obediently, Matilda drank deeply. As she set the cup on the floor, the door opened and Roger entered, followed by a sullen-looking Howard. His straw-coloured hair poked out from below his hat in all directions, topping a pale face, the skin of which stretched to accommodate the fat that filled his cheeks. He must have been the last fat man in the county. Somehow, Howard always had enough to eat, but never enough to share. And his last meal usually adorned his clothes. Since he'd become reeve to Lord Robert de Ayermin's estate, he'd swollen with further self-importance. Matilda shuddered. He'd been full of sunshine when they were children and used to follow her about like a puppy. Then when he realised she was promised to Galeran, and that was a promise she intended to keep, resentment extinguished the sunshine.

'My sorrow for your loss. May Galeran enjoy eternal life,' Howard said, unconvincingly.

The mention of Galeran's name stung Matilda. She opened her mouth as if to object but Roger held up his hand. 'A cart won't move through the mud. Thom is a fine horse but he needs to be fresh for working later. We can't risk tiring him.'

'It'll not tire him to go such a short distance,' Matilda said peevishly.

'But it will tire him to work for all who ask the lend of him. And today it will be hard to say no. I'll return shortly.'

Matilda opened her mouth to argue but swiftly closed it, realising Roger was right. She wasn't in a fit mind to say no to anyone. And they would ask. Someone would ask. There was always work a horse would make easier, but it would be up to Matilda to find the extra feed Thom would need, and there was little enough as it was.

Roger retreated and closed the door gently.

'Sit,' said Maerwynn. 'Save your strength.'

Matilda nodded and returned to sit at Maerwynn's feet. 'I thought we'd have to bury him without church,' she said.

'There's always a priest to be bought,' Maerwynn said in a matter-of-fact tone. 'He'll be rubbing his hands now, contemplating the profit he will make today.'

Matilda's eyes widened. She hadn't thought of payment.

As if reading her mind, Maerwynn continued, 'That is not for you to fret about. Roger will make an arrangement.'

'I shall be heavily indebted.'

'And there will be a time for you to repay your debt – but not today.'

She would repay her debt – if she lived long enough. When the rains began last spring, they'd all grumbled good-heartedly, relieved that the late hard frosts and their accompanying flurries of sleet and hailstones had ceased. Last year's piercing winds had brought in their wake a hot dry summer that baked the chalk ground bone-hard. They were still ploughing in October, struggling to save what they could of the meagre harvest. People went hungry to feed their oxen and horses, and to pay for new ploughboards and buy ale for the ploughmen. But there had been bad harvests before. They'd manage somehow.

The grain couldn't ripen and good bread had become scarce. A luxury. Prices had been high before but the villagers hadn't known they were blessed. Scarcity drove the costs of even the most basic things to a level beyond the means of many. From spring to midsummer, prices had risen until they'd doubled or more. The King's orders to hold prices down had no power when hungry traders refused to listen.

No one had expected the rain to fall for so long when it finally arrived that autumn.

Matilda dreaded ever having to go to market again. Following the long path that avoided the steep climb of Giant's Grave Hill, it rose and dipped as if by a whim. All looked so much bleaker from higher ground. The downs looked grey and brown – not green as they should have;

the colours had been washed away by the rain and only the harsh and tangled gorse seemed to survive. The trees in the forest drooped, bringing her heart down. Instead of feeling the bounce of new life beneath her steps, she had to drag her feet through mud and flint. And she watched her feet not simply to save herself from a fall, but also because the longer she looked across the downs, the sadder the land seemed to grow.

Even the costs of pots and urns had risen as everyone sought to dry what they could indoors. And salt – they fought over what they bought from passing pedlars. There was hardly enough to preserve all the meat. Roger had told Matilda that he'd seen beasts left to litter the fields when he walked with the sheep. His flock was small compared to many – some owned hundreds of sheep. Usually, the dry higher land kept them safe from foot rot, but not anymore. They cast their beady eyes on passers-by as if to let them know that they owned the land. But all the flocks were fast shrinking. And more and more were being claimed by the rivers that surrounded their lands. With rising waters sheep would tumble in when they sought a drink, weighed down by their heavy coats to their fast-flowing death. Things hadn't got so bad in their village – yet. But when people passed through, the villagers measured them according to the size of their bellies and thanked God when they moved on.

And as if hunger weren't enough, as if the constant growl of their bellies and the cries of children tugging at their heartstrings was somehow insufficient, pestilence had followed close behind. Maerwynn had wept when she delivered the first dead child. By the fifth she was thanking God for taking it early.

Galeran had succumbed to the pestilence. Others had, too. A few left fearfully under cover of night, taking what money and valuables they could to pay their way, but there was nowhere to run from this. Father Luke had been one such. He'd emptied the church's coffers and disappeared three weeks ago. No one knew where. No one now cared.

Maerwynn stood and poured two cups of ale, handing one to Matilda. 'Drink,' she said. 'Roger will soon return.'

Obediently, Matilda drank deeply. As she set the cup on the floor, the door opened and Roger entered, followed by a sullen-looking Howard. His straw-coloured hair poked out from below his hat in all directions, topping a pale face, the skin of which stretched to accommodate the fat that filled his cheeks. He must have been the last fat man in the county. Somehow, Howard always had enough to eat, but never enough to share. And his last meal usually adorned his clothes. Since he'd become reeve to Lord Robert de Ayermin's estate, he'd swollen with further self-importance. Matilda shuddered. He'd been full of sunshine when they were children and used to follow her about like a puppy. Then when he realised she was promised to Galeran, and that was a promise she intended to keep, resentment extinguished the sunshine.

'My sorrow for your loss. May Galeran enjoy eternal life,' Howard said, unconvincingly.

Matilda didn't bother to respond. 'Shall we leave now?' she asked Roger.

Roger signalled Howard who looked over at Galeran's corpse, an expression of distaste crossing his face. 'Lift his feet,' he said to Howard, 'and I'll take the other end. Matilda, you and Maerwynn can follow us.'

Howard shrugged. 'Very well. 'Tis from the goodness of my heart that I act as your labouring man.'

Huffing and puffing, Howard did as he'd been instructed and he and Roger left the house. As Matilda stepped outside, she saw her neighbours standing with heads bowed. *There but for the grace of God …*

Slowly, they made their way to the church at the edge of the village of Oare. It was only a few minutes' walk, but it felt like the longest walk Matilda had ever taken. Howard huffed and puffed, letting Roger bear most of Galeran's weight. The mud squelched beneath their feet and splattered up their straining legs despite their efforts to seek drier ground – there was none.

Matilda gasped as Roger stumbled, nearly dropping Galeran. *No!* That would be an indignity too great to bear. Galeran would be covered in mud the moment he hit the ground. Roger gave a determined gasp and regained his footing, turning to offer Matilda a woeful glance.

None of the villagers had followed them. Matilda turned and looked back. She'd expected no more. In days past, the whole village would have been present at a funeral. It wouldn't have mattered if they liked the family, or even if they were friendly with them. But there'd been too many of late – and it was common knowledge that Galeran had died from a pestilence. A pestilence that Matilda might be carrying within. She sighed; it would be done soon.

Maerwynn slipped her arm around Matilda's waist as if she could read her thoughts. She had been such a comfort these last days. But that was what Maerwynn was – a comfort for all the villagers in their times of trial. She was a short, stocky woman, some years older than Matilda and they'd become friends as soon as Maerwynn had arrived in the village five years ago. No one knew what lay in her past or from which family she came, but as time went on, people stopped asking the questions she answered only with a smile. It wasn't important. She was one of them now.

'Make haste,' called out the young priest Roger had summoned as soon as they were within earshot. He stood at the door of the church, hopping from foot to foot, impatiently. 'I have to return for another burial in Marlborough, before this day is done.' He belched and flushed bright red.

Roger and Howard pushed past the priest and delivered Galeran into the church. In a haze, Matilda followed and stood huddled with the others as the priest muttered unintelligibly. She grabbed Roger's sleeve. 'Who will dig the grave?' she whispered.

'It's done,' said Roger in a low voice, patting her hand.

Then Maerwynn tugged at her arm. 'Come,' she said. 'We're going to bury him now.'

A moment later Matilda was standing next to a shallow grave, watching as Howard and Roger lowered Galeran into it with as much reverence as they could muster. She tossed in the rosemary. The priest muttered quickly, and within what seemed only moments Roger was shovelling mud on top of Galeran's corpse. Matilda glanced round. To her surprise, she saw Adam standing a few yards away, head bowed. He seemed so young to be a squire – it wasn't so long ago that Galeran had climbed a tree to help him down when he'd frozen with fear at the top, so entranced by the shiny red apples above that he hadn't realised how high he was until he looked down. Lord Robert wasn't present, but he didn't need to be with Howard as his representative.

A young woman approached Adam and leaned towards him to whisper in his ear. Matilda's eyes widened. *Lady Adelaide?*

She realised Roger had said something. 'I'm sorry – what did you say?' she asked.

'The priest is leaving,' Roger said.

Matilda nodded and turned away as the priest walked towards her, hand held out in front of him.

Maerwynn shuffled closer and put an arm around Matilda's shoulders. 'It's right to weep,' she said.

'I have no tears left,' said Matilda. Lest she sounded dismissive, she offered Maerwynn a wan smile. 'I think I need some sleep.'

Maerwynn nodded. 'We can go back now if you wish.'

Roger was still attempting to move mud. Howard had

disappeared from sight, eager to relinquish the task he clearly believed to be below his station. Matilda looked towards Adam and he offered her a brief wave before walking away. Lady Adelaide was nowhere to be seen. Perhaps Matilda had imagined her being there.

Maerwynn pulled at Matilda's arm and they slowly walked back towards her house. 'I know what you're fretting about,' said Maerwynn briskly.

'And that is?' Matilda offered without really caring.

'There isn't enough food to share. No one will think badly of you.'

'Roger brought me some cheese yesterday. And I have saved a morsel of bread.'

'You must eat it.'

'Will you share it with me? It's no more than a token but at least us two can eat in Galeran's honour,' Matilda said, although she thought it odd to mark Galeran's death with the human necessity that had killed him.

'No one expects a wake meal in these times. There is no shame,' said Maerwynn firmly. She halted and took Matilda's hand, her voice softening. 'You don't want to be alone? I will sit with you awhile, but then I must attend to Beth. She nears her confinement. And you should rest.'

They reached the house and Matilda put her hand on the door. She paused. 'The cuckoo didn't sing,' she said. 'Did you hear a cuckoo?'

Maerwynn shook her head. 'He'll only sing when fair weather is coming.'

'In other years he would sing today.'

'This is not like other years.'

'There'll be no cuckoo king this year,' mused Matilda.

Maerwynn laughed. 'We have more to worry about than cuckoos. Come, let's go inside.'

Matilda smiled for the first time that day. She opened the door and waved Maerwynn ahead of her.

The sky did not weep that morning. And neither did Matilda.

CHAPTER 2

End of April 1314

Three musicians! One banging a drum, another sounding a trumpet and the third playing a lute. They reached the green and paused. Doors opened as villagers came out to see what was going on. The musicians watched as everyone moved towards them and stood in wait.

The drummer sounded a rat-a-tat-tat and went silent again. A young woman ran towards the musicians and stood next to them. She was clearly one of their party as they turned to smile at her. The drummer went rat-a-tat-tat again. The villagers surged forward. They froze as the young woman bowed deeply, extended her hands widely to indicate the musicians and opened her mouth wide with joy.

The whole village sighed as her sweet voice floated in the air and danced among the clouds. The drummer lightly tapped out a beat and the trumpeter blew softly. A moment later the lutist began to strum and the woman sang more loudly, more strongly. And the villagers sighed again.

When the song was completed, the villagers whooped and cheered. And those few who hadn't ventured out feared they were missing something and exited their homes grumbling and complaining. One woman appeared with a baby stuck firmly on her breast and clucking at three earnest looking young children who lined up behind her.

With a flourish the trumpeter ran to her side, bowed and blew a loud blast towards her. She giggled and jumped backwards, almost knocking down the children who stared wide-eyed. Then he bowed and offered his arm. The woman bowed back and accepted it and he led her to the middle of the green.

Matilda felt a pull at her skirts. 'Man has taken Mama,' said the boy with a grave expression on his face. 'Is that a bad man?'

Matilda smiled at him. 'I don't believe so. You can wait and watch.'

The boy nodded and grabbed his sister's hand. In turn, she grabbed their youngest brother's hand. They all shifted slightly to make it clear they were standing next to Matilda and looked up at her hopefully.

'Watch,' she said, although she had no more idea than anyone else what they were watching.

'I see Kate is at the centre of it all again,' Roger leaned over and whispered in her ear.

Matilda jumped. She hadn't known he was there. Before she could respond, the drummer quickly played a roll and shouted for attention. The woman who had been singing held out her hands and nodded at Kate who hesitated and then pulled the baby from her breast, hastily covering herself. The baby let out a wail, stopping immediately as the woman began singing to him in a low voice.

The lutist began to play and the drummer tapped out a rhythm. The trumpeter offered Kate another low bow and took her hand. He began to lead her in a series of steps. Laughing, she followed his lead, watching his feet closely. After a couple of stumbling rounds she became more confident, and the trumpeter, sensing this, began to whirl her here and there, in one circle and another.

The music grew louder and a couple stepped forward. The crowd cheered as they began to sip and whirl. And another and another until the green was filled with whooshing skirts and twirling bodies.

'Do you wish to dance?' asked Roger.

'I don't think your wife would like that,' said Matilda absently. She realised what she had said and slapped her hand across her mouth. It had only been three months since Marion had died in childbirth, her baby lasting only a few hours more. 'Oh! I'm so sorry, Roger. I wasn't thinking.'

Roger shrugged. 'I forget too. Sometimes I come back from the fields and call out for her. And when I wake in the morning, I reach out and wonder where she is.'

Matilda patted his arm in sympathy. Roger rarely spoke of Marion and her words would make his wound cut no less deeply. He stared into the distance and Matilda watched him for a moment and turned back towards the dancing.

Suddenly, it was over. The music stopped and the dancers began to move away.

Matilda felt another tug at her skirts. 'Will Mama come back now?' the boy asked.

'Yes,' said Roger before Matilda could respond. 'Would you like to reward the musicians?' he added as he produced a coin and handed it to the boy. 'Go. Give it to the trumpeter.'

Kate was talking animatedly to the trumpeter with her baby held over her shoulder. She shrieked when her children approached and they ran to her and flung their arms around her. The boy with the coin disentangled himself and turned to offer his payment to the trumpeter. He was rewarded with a loud parrp! and offered a huge grin in return. Following his lead, other villagers offered coins as payment and someone brought over jugs of ale for the musicians.

'It looks as if they plan to stay,' observed Roger. 'Good. May Day will be much better with their music.' He looked around. 'Do you know where Galeran is? He offered his help in putting up the maypole.'

Matilda shook her head. 'I haven't seen him these last two days. He went into town with his father.'

Roger hissed in annoyance. 'I'll find someone else to help. Have you finished the garlands?'

'We have enough garlands at home for three villages!' said Matilda. 'I had to stop my mother from making more. There is so much blossom everywhere, it's hard to move.'

'It will be a good May Day, even if it does rain again.'

15

Roger gave Matilda a serious look. 'You don't sound very happy. It's an honour to be Queen.'

Matilda grinned. 'So Mama keeps telling me.'

She looked around. The musicians had now disappeared, presumably to Agnes's where they could avail themselves of more ale and find a bed for a night or two. Everyone else was now going about their daily tasks as usual. 'And she will be wondering where I am.'

'Go. I will see you in the morning.'

Matilda turned away and then as an afterthought she called back over her shoulder, 'Galeran will be there. He wouldn't miss this.'

Roger didn't respond so she turned back to face him. He stood rigid, deep in thought. 'He wouldn't miss this,' she repeated.

'I pray not,' Roger said. 'He will make a good Robin Goodfellow for his Queen.'

'Yes,' Matilda said without conviction.

Roger raised his eyebrows. 'It is rightful. You and Galeran have been promised for so long.'

'Yes.' Matilda looked carefully at a spot on the ground.

'Though you are the Queen of the May and can marry anyone,' Roger said slowly.

'But it will be Galeran I marry,' Matilda said flatly.

'Anyone,' insisted Roger.

'But it will be Galeran,' she said with a polite smile.

CHAPTER 3

Late May 1316

This year there was no gathering to welcome the spring. The spring didn't appear to want a welcome. By now, the May tree's white blossom and red berries should be signalling hope. In past years, Galeran had gathered knots of blossom and presented them shyly to Matilda who'd bowed her head with mock seriousness before accepting them. In past years, villagers ran across the fields, basking in the spring sun and playing games with ball and stick.

The May tree's hedges marked more than boundaries between field, hill and forest. The copses that ran alongside the rivers stood guard on the edges between water and land, on the boundary of this world and another. And the sarsen stones did more than hold the land together, they confined dark magic that tried to escape – or so it was said.

There was too much sorrow to romp and cavort, too much death. Only yesterday Walter had gasped his last. And he'd been such a young man, with a wife and three children, all tiny. The living were hardly sufficient to bury the dead. Roger refused to dig Walter's grave. He'd already dug three in the last fortnight and he daren't leave the sheep unattended again. The last time he'd done so, two lambs had disappeared. The sheep and cattle were falling prey to the pestilence without such theft, and too many calves were being born dead.

At least someone would have a full belly. There was little meat to be had. Strangers had passed through the village bringing tales of fat dogs being stolen to eat. And stories of the starving secretly eating their own children's flesh – not that they had met such people or would think of doing so themselves, but it must have happened, it was said so often. Once the strangers found there was no work to be had and no food to be shared, they moved on until another group arrived, telling the same tales.

It wasn't the hunger alone that caused Death's sickle to fall. Fever had swept through the village on more than one occasion. Damp grain fell corrupt; mildew coated the scrawny fruit. While one man vomited all he ate, another wailed that it charged through his body in moments only to emerge at the other end as a foul-smelling slurry. And they were still hungry.

Someone needed to dig Walter's grave and the men were all in the fields, so Matilda and Maerwynn took up spades and dug while Walter's wife watched and sobbed. Her cheeks were sunken and her colour pallid. Matilda reckoned she would be reunited with her husband soon, then wondered if the same would be true for her.

She shuddered. 'I don't want to fall like the others.' She thought, 'I won't.' The children stood next to her, silent in their confusion, thin as twigs. It was cold, too cold for May. But blessedly the rain had ceased a few days earlier so the mud no longer battled against the spade.

Matilda stayed silent. There were no words that had not already been said. And it was over soon enough. She raised her eyebrows at Maerwynn who nodded and followed her back to the house. Walter's widow's wails followed them.

'Oof,' said Maerwynn as she collapsed onto the bed. 'I can't remember the last time I had a good night's sleep. If it isn't dreaming of pudding, it's a bang on the door asking for herbs or hand-holding. As if a herb is more effective at night!'

A mouse emerged from the mattress and scurried across Maerwynn's skirts. She ignored it. Matilda hissed in annoyance. She thought she'd shaken them all out the day before.

'I'm going to Wootton Rivers tomorrow,' said Matilda. 'Will you come with me?'

'I can't. I have to go to the manor. Lady Adelaide is suffering from the flux and wants some potion to plug it. I should have gone today, but death trumps all. Anyway, where did you get the money? Did Galeran have a hidden hoard?'

Matilda laughed. 'Galeran couldn't hide anything. Whatever he did was written on his face. No, I'm selling, not buying. Onions are making good money now and I have more than I need. And I haven't yet sold Galeran's clothes. They must be worth something.' She paused before saying worriedly, 'Is there now pestilence in the manor?'

Maerwynn made a dismissive motion. 'If there is, they're keeping it quiet. Last time she called on me was because her bowels were stopped. She thinks too much of her innards. They don't interest me as much as she believes.'

'Maerwynn!' Matilda said wide-eyed.

'It's true! But she thinks too much in all ways. She reads and summons scholars – strange looking men – to tell her more things to think about.'

'I wish I had enough time to sit and think.'

Maerwynn sat upright and regarded Matilda. 'I've seen little of you these last weeks. Your burden is heavy.'

Matilda shrugged. 'I have it better than some. My garden is yielding some produce and I am rebuilding my stores. It's so quiet without Galeran. He was always there.'

'The love of your life.'

Matilda paused. 'Not like in the ballads,' she said, finally. 'Not a love like that. As I said, he was always there. It was how it was meant to be. A good arrangement, a happy arrangement.'

'Few of us have a love like in the ballads. Not I,' said Maerwynn. 'That isn't real life.'

'I thought it was a good enough life,' said Matilda. 'But after everything I am not sure what I want.'

Maerwynn nodded slowly and to Matilda's surprise she threw her arms around her and engulfed her in a tight hug. 'All things can be worked out with enough time.'

CHAPTER 4

April 1315

Galeran looked so pleased with himself it made Matilda smile. She raised her hand in greeting as he approached. With a sigh hissing from her lips, she rubbed her back. It was only a small garden but she'd spent so many hours the last few weeks tending to it. At least the carrots looked like they'd grow strong. And the apple tree was covered in blossom despite having been bare until the week before. It was an old, strong tree and wouldn't be diverted from producing its bounty no matter the weather.

Splashes of mud adorned Galeran's grey stockings and his red tunic, now much faded by the sun, was covered in leaves and twigs as if he'd recently crawled under a hedge. Knowing Galeran, that was precisely what had happened. Why walk the long way around when wriggling on the ground could save you twenty minutes or more?

'The sun hasn't yet gone down,' called Matilda. 'I thought you'd be much longer. You should have ridden.'

She shivered. A bitter chill was rising in the air – far

too bitter for this time of year. Matilda pulled her skirts more tightly around herself. She glanced into the distance, a mist was forming around the base of Giant's Grave Hill, she recalled the tales of its treacherous nature. People often spoke of the hill having a will of its own, and beasts that wander in the mists that so often coat the Downs. Matilda found this fanciful, but thought it prudent not to tempt fate and wander in their looking for trouble.

'The day was fine and I didn't need to hurry,' Galeran said briskly as he dropped a sack at Matilda's feet. 'There! I have candles. And some salt. And I bought almonds.' He raised his eyebrows. 'You would weep if I told you how much I paid for those.'

'Those are all small things,' Matilda said as she pulled at the twine that sealed the sack. 'What more do you hide in here?'

Galeran hopped from foot to foot, still grinning. 'Take it inside,' he said. 'I need to sit and quench my thirst.'

Matilda let go of the sack and patted Galeran's hand. 'Come. Maerwynn brought some ale.'

'I thought we already had plenty of ale,' Galeran said in confusion.

'We did have plenty, but it has been a long day. I may have drunk more than I should have,' Matilda said with a grin. 'And mine is never as good as Maerwynn's. There's a little cheese left and I made bread just after you left. Were there crowds?' She turned to their cottage and pushed the door open.

Theirs was one of the older cottages. It was made of

solid stone and its single room ended in a half partition in front of a byre where an angry looking goat stared at two urns that had the temerity to stand before it. The chickens attacked their ankles as they entered and Matilda waved her arms to waft them away. To no avail – they returned almost immediately.

A rope bed topped with a straw mattress lay against the left wall with a curtain hung before it to separate it from the rest of the room. Matilda leaned across it and pushed the window shutters further open to claim the last of the light. Absent-mindedly, she kicked at a chicken and it immediately released a loud squawk.

Galeran pulled Matilda to his chest and kissed her briefly before dropping to the floor in front of the fire, rubbing his hands.

Matilda opened the sack and gasped. 'A rabbit? You bought a rabbit at the market?'

'No. I saw Roger on the way back. He had three and told me to take one for the cheese you gave him last month. It will make a fine meal.'

Matilda's mouth watered. Cheese making was late this year and it was scarce. And the pottage was now more water than anything – a rabbit in the pot would make more than a fine meal for the next two days. She immediately fetched the knife and dropped the rabbit onto the table to skin it.

'Come sit with me awhile,' said Galeran. 'You can do that later. A few minutes will make little difference.'

'Aren't you hungry?'

'More hungry for you,' Galeran said impishly.

Matilda laughed, wiping her long fingers on a clean rag and left the rabbit on the table, its glazed eyes staring at the roof. She took hold of the jug and poured a cup of ale, handing it to Galeran before she took one for herself and sat down next to him. 'Were there crowds?' she asked again.

'Like you wouldn't believe. So many people chattering and pushing. They fear there won't be enough food. The prices! So much for fixing them. But I made a few coins selling that kindling. And I played under the cross.' With a flourish, Galeran pulled his flute from under his tunic and held it aloft. 'People will always pay for a tune.'

'And did you hear anything of interest?'

'Old Martin – you remember him? That miserable man with the long hair and no teeth who grumbled all the time? He used to live next to the church before he went to stay with his daughter in town.'

Matilda nodded. 'Miserable old soul. I heard his daughter tried to hide when he arrived at her door.'

'He died last week. He was wretched drunk after selling in Marlborough, and kicked out of an alehouse, somewhere to the north. He'd taken a short cut over Giant's Hill and was found the next day, body broken.'

'No!' Matilda shook her head. 'That shows his complaints were heard, at least.'

'His misery made him fall?'

'His misery made him foolhardy enough to take that road.'

24

Galeran raised his eyebrows but didn't wait for a further response.

All who lived in the heart of the Wessex Downs knew how treacherous many of the hills and crevasses were. Only a fool or a desperate man would take those roads at night. The steep banks rose to the sky; to climb one was to climb a wall, peppered with low wide sarsen stones the paths offered no guidance.

'And Lord Robert's household fell prey to a pestilence a few days ago. That's why we haven't seen any of them. They have enough to eat but it goes in one end, and straight out the other. They say the stink starts ten feet before you enter the door.'

'Poor things.'

'Nothing poor about them.' He let out a sigh and took a swig of his ale. Then he continued to chatter – he must have spoken to nearly everyone at the market! That wasn't unusual. Galeran was easy to speak to and interested in everyone and everything. And his flute was enough to break any ice that might remain.

Matilda busied herself preparing the rabbit. Before long, it boiled over the fire.

'Did you see Maerwynn today?' asked Galeran.

'Yes, I told you. She brought some ale over. And she said Beth is near her time.'

'Already? Is that her third?'

'Her fourth,' Matilda said absentmindedly.

Galeran looked at her carefully and paused before speaking. 'We've only been married for a few months.

There is time.' He reassured her, not understanding her dismissal of the talk of babies.

It had only been a few months but it felt as if they'd been married forever. Probably because they'd known each other since they could walk. There was never any question about who either of them would marry. Others had parents making frenzied arrangements when they approached full age. Sending messages to this village and that. Matilda's and Galeran's parents simply shrugged, accepting the inevitable. Sadly, Matilda's mother had died in the hard winter last year – her father had been long gone; she could barely remember him. Galeran had also lost his mother to the hard weather, although his father still lived at the other end of the village. He was a bad-tempered soul. It was as if Galeran had created his own sunny disposition as an antidote to his father's misery.

Any child of Galeran's would surely be as sunny. Matilda knew this, but was conflicted. She always felt as though she *should* want children rather than actually wanting them as other women did.

'And maybe it's a good thing,' continued Galeran. 'With the bad weather and the small harvests, maybe our children are waiting. They'll arrive when they know they'll have full bellies and not have the damp creep into their bones.'

Galeran was right. Now was not a good time to bring a child into the world. And once a child did arrive, there would no doubt be another and then another and her life would be made of children alone. That's if she lived through each confinement. 'It was a blessing babies didn't want to come,' she secretly thought but would never say for fear of upsetting Galeran; he so wanted them. Though if she didn't have them, what would she do with her days as she became older.

'We won't have another year like the last one,' added Galeran.

'Things might not change that quickly,' said Matilda. 'Let's eat and you can tell me a tale.'

Galeran sat placidly while Matilda prepared their meal. He told her of the people he'd spoken to, who was well, who was ill. And of the pompous priest who'd been walking through the market square when a young boy had laid a rope across his path so he tumbled upside down and showed how little he wore beneath his robes. Galeran sniggered at the memory. 'It seems so long ago that I was a young boy playing such tricks,' he said. 'People like that need cutting down to size once in a while. Though I never looked as innocent as that boy.'

The smell from the cooking pot made their mouths water long before the food was ready. The moment Matilda judged the rabbit cooked, she served two large portions into bowls and set them on the table.

'No,' said Galeran. 'It's too cold. Let's eat by the fire.'

Matilda retrieved the bowls and they sat huddled before the flames. Once they'd eaten their fill in silence, Galeran set down his bowl and pulled Matilda close to him.

'And now your tale?' asked Matilda.

'Why not? I heard this tale from that old woman who sells the candles,' Galeran said. He batted a chicken away. It ran into the corner as if he'd set it on fire and began to gossip loudly with the other two chickens that sat there watching them attentively.

Matilda snuggled close to Galeran.

'They say there is a puck awake in the woods between the church and the river,' he said. 'He's been there for generations but is usually no bother.'

'How do they know he is there?'

'Sometimes he helps in the fields, in the dead of night when all are sleeping. They wake to find that morning's tasks already complete. Sometimes he mills corn or makes cheese in the night to save us from work. Or he comes to the house and cleans and will return if he's paid with milk or honey.'

'He hasn't been here,' Matilda said ruefully, glancing around the room. 'What does he look like?'

'He is very, very old. Sometimes he comes as a beast, like a man with a tail, covered in hair. At others he takes the shape of a raven, a fox or a goat. No matter what shape he takes, his fur is dark. And his eyes have a golden glow.'

Matilda closed her eyes for a moment to picture the beast.

'And,' Galeran continued, 'he warns away travellers who have ill intent. He may offer a ride on his back and will charge hither and thither until fear makes your heart fair leave your breast. But he'll deliver you back safely.' He leaned closer to Matilda as if to share a secret. 'There was a man who'd beaten another till he almost met his death and he'd run and run until he reached our village. He was weary when a pony appeared and offered him a ride to the next town.'

'He didn't question his ears? You would question me if I said that Thom had spoken.'

Galeran laughed. 'He was surprised to hear words from a pony's mouth but too tired after nearly killing a man to wonder much.'

'Did he accept the ride?'

'He did. And it began well. But then the pony ran faster and faster. It didn't matter what the man did, the pony had decided to run. So the man clung on for fear of his life, whipped by branches and stabbed by thorns as the pony charged through the woods as if the trees were of no consequence. The birds fled from the trees shrieking in terror. Squirrels ran into holes. And the pony still ran. Finally, it shook itself hard and threw the man to the ground. Afeared, he hid in a ditch until the pony was gone. At the dead of night, he walked to the next town. He told an alewife of his trials and she offered him a drink, saying that he should never travel that way again. And the man sighed once and fell to the floor, dead.'

'When did this happen?'

'Near the end of winter. The puck usually sleeps now and through the summer. But there were too few crops to leave him his share in the last harvest and his belly has rumbled him awake.'

'And he makes mischief?'

'When he's bored. If you offend him, he'll chase you down and drink your blood before he eats you. But if he meets someone with a good soul, he leads them from harm. He has his own rules. But if you fear him, cold iron will protect you.'

Matilda laughed. 'I will carry the cooking pot with me if I need venture near the woods alone.'

Galeran nodded. 'It would be well to do that.'

'So has the chandler's wife seen him?'

'She has seen many things through her ale-aided eyes. Many strange things. But she has not yet seen a puck. Though she said she knows someone who has.'

Matilda yawned. 'You will give me bad dreams.'

Galeran stood and pulled Matilda to her feet. 'It grows dark. Come with me to bed. Let me make good dreams for you.'

CHAPTER 5

September 1316

In the woods between the church and the river, a little east of the mossy bank and down by the blackberry thicket, lay an old path. It led nowhere – at least, nowhere that anyone wished to go. It had become overgrown through years of neglect and the ebbing of memory had almost hidden it, but it never went back to the forest entirely. Every village child had once followed it in curiosity and succumbed to disappointment when it ended in a dip with two tall oak trees standing as sentries beside it. The dip was bare as if the grass and flowers found it too tiresome to try to cover it. The trees looked tired, old, as if they wouldn't last another winter. But each winter they did, for longer than anyone could remember.

If those children had bothered, they could have inspected the dip more closely and they would have found that it extended beneath the tree to the left and revealed an opening to a black pit. Perhaps some had bothered, but the opening looked as if it might house all manner of devils. It was better not to awaken them, or draw attention by talking about them.

But tonight, in the deepest part of the night, that hour of darkness before dawn, something moved and scraped and sighed from the pit. The moon was so thin, so weak that its meagre light couldn't penetrate the blanket of cloud. The stars were obscured.

And with the movement, the sentry trees wept greatly. They wept as trees do by dropping leaves and sprinkling buds. They wept for their loss. They wept because if it left, if they were alone again, they would drift into a slumber.

With a sigh it emerged from the pit. It stood and shook itself gently. Then it tapped one of the trees, causing a flurry of leaves to drop to the ground.

The beast stood tall. Its back was studded, and its huge round head contained two horns that pointed to where the moon should be. It snapped its large teeth. It shook itself and smoothed the thick black fur that covered its body. It yawned.

A soft rain coated the beast with droplets and it stuck its tongue out to catch them. The beast gave a shiver and a shake so strong that the sentry trees shook and nearly cried out. Then the beast was a man, standing in the trees.

Finn dropped down to the ground and scurried into the pit. A moment later he emerged with a sack. He upended it and snatched up the tunic and breeches that fell out. Quickly, he dressed himself.

An owl flew down onto a nearby thornbush where it sat precariously and stared at Finn with curiosity. Finn bared his teeth with a grin, the owl screeched but held its place. And the clouds parted and a sliver of light shone down and lit up Finn's amber eyes. The owl screeched again, more loudly. Apparently deciding retreat was the better part of valour, it extended its wings and soared into the sky.

Finn laughed. He picked up the sack and flung it over his shoulder. Whistling softly, he began to follow the path out of the woods and towards the village.

CHAPTER 6

Winter 1315

Hunger has its own hierarchy. Some are destined to fade away alone, no tears shed for them. Others share what little they have – mothers say they need less so they can give their share to their children. And some offer their last withered apple to the old woman along the lane who can no longer see more than mist, remembering how she'd helped them when they were young. Most are fair and take care of their stores but also make sure their neighbours don't suffer too much.

But a few – not few enough – jealously guard what they have. They take what isn't rightfully theirs if the opportunity presents itself and they deny they have flour or corn remaining. They place themselves above others. Those of the church need to be well fed; how else could they do God's work?

Father James always looked well. He had ruddy cheeks and a satisfied smirk on his face no matter what the season. Long before the hunger had visited, he'd learned the ways in which a priest could take according to his pleasure. His taking was not only of this material world; he laid claims to skills he didn't possess and talents that were beyond him. But most of all, he took advantage.

Since they'd been small boys, Galeran and his younger brother Audri had incurred Father James's wrath. Sometimes, it was their own fault. They jumped on any opportunity to embarrass the priest. Whether it was placing something in his way so he tripped head over heels or – as they grew older – repeating the priest's more outlandish claims where he might be challenged, they found ample opportunity to cause embarrassment. The villagers never forgot the occasion when a visitor was informed by Audri in wide-eyed innocence that Father James was an expert piper but lacked an instrument. The visitor immediately proffered his own flute. Father James blustered for a moment before having to admit he knew no more than which way up to hold it. After that, whenever Father James wanted someone to blame, he'd look to Audri and Galeran.

As they grew into adulthood, Audri and Galeran spent less time together. Even less once Galeran and Matilda were betrothed. Audri had no sweetheart. He spent most of his time with Simon and John, loud-mouthed youths who had no time for Galeran. In time, Audri became as loud as his companions.

There were soon whispers. Small items went missing whenever the boys were there. A loaf of bread here, a coin there. Always small things and always at times when other explanations were possible. But it happened much too often to be coincidence. And none of them could hold their ale. At least once a week, they tore through the village, laughing raucously, kicking aside anything in their path and emptying their bellies of drink and their last meal on their neighbours' doorsteps.

Usually, the boys' antics received no more than exasperation. After all, they'd all been young once and grown out of their foolishness. But when the hunger came, people began to lock away their stores and keep closer account of what they owned. Audri and his friends saw no sport in such thefts any longer.

It was early winter when two men arrived in the village and went to stay at Father James's home. After one night, they left, only to return a few days later, one carrying a bundle under his arms. And the same happened again. One fine morning, Audri stopped them on the road and asked where they were heading.

'The abbey up yonder,' the shorter of the two said, pointing west. He was a thin, weasely-looking youth of around Audri's age. His companion was as thin but had a pleasant countenance, with a broad smile fixed to his face.

'And you'll return again soon?'

The weasel man shrugged. 'If there's a message to return,' he said. 'Or we might go elsewhere.'

It transpired that they made a living by carrying messages and letters between clergy. Sometimes they simply memorised what was to be said. And they kept in their heads anything that might be useful. They passed through the village every few days and Audri and his friends fell to sharing an ale or two with them each time. Before long, the men told of the richness of food in the monasteries, how the abbeys held bottles of fine wines and rich bread while villagers starved. And how for indulgences Father James shared in this bounty. They told good tales.

'But it isn't as it was. With the lack of harvest, even the monks have begun to suffer.'

This was why Audri knew who was responsible when stores were broken into, chickens disappeared and cheeses vanished. Each time the men passed through, Audri and his friends were blamed. In exasperation, Audri sought Galeran's advice.

'You can understand why,' Galeran said. 'Your past sins are haunting you.'

'But things are different now!'

'Do Simon and John think the same?'

'I'd lay my life on it.'

Galeran believed Audri and went to speak to Father James. Before he opened his mouth, the priest said, 'I haven't seen you at Mass this last fortnight.'

'I had to work the fields,' Galeran said shortly before explaining his errand.

Father James shrugged. 'That's a dangerous accusation to make against men of God. Has anyone seen what you say has happened?'

'Not exactly, but who else would it be?'

Galeran was about to add more but Father James held up his hand to silence him. 'I don't want to hear it. You've always let your mouth run ahead of your mind, Galeran. And you have no proof. These men are on important business and need to be allowed to carry out their tasks unimpeded.' Father James turned away and Galeran left, full of frustration.

Audri shrugged when Galeran related the conversation. 'That isn't the way to resolve it. We need to catch them in the act.'

'It won't go well, even if you do,' said Galeran. 'The church looks after its own.' He paused. 'Share a meal with us tonight. You haven't been to my house for weeks now.'

Matilda was surprised when Galeran returned with Audri but decided that their meal would stretch to one more mouth. When they'd finished eating, Galeran played his flute for a while, then the three of them huddled in front of the fire.

'It's raining heavily,' Matilda observed. 'It might be as well to spend the night here.' She looked upon Audri as a brother and loved him dearly.

Audri nodded and yawned. 'My thanks for the meal.'

'Father James is no doubt nursing a full belly,' said Galeran. 'The church takes too much.'

'It's always been that way,' said Matilda.

'Not always. Not so much.'

'As long as I can remember, anyway.'

38

Audri wriggled to get more comfortable, between his brother and sister-in-law. 'The world isn't going to change with people being so hungry.'

Galeran shook his head. 'People being hungry is why it should change. The tithe barns are full. The damp is causing wheat to rot while people go hungry. And the monks and priests gorge themselves while demanding more. And every day Father James asks more money for his indulgences. What use is a God that only cares for those with a bottomless purse?'

'Money gets rid of sin,' said Audri. 'You don't need a church for that. It would happen, anyway.'

'But they don't live to our rules,' continued Galeran. 'It's more than the money. They tell us what we should do to live a good life but they do as they will.' He sighed glumly and stared into the fire. 'In the old times people worked side by side. High or low born they acted to the same rules.'

'The old rules still apply,' said Matilda. 'There's more to the world than men bring.' She nudged Galeran. 'Tell us a tale before we sleep. Tell us a tale of the old times.'

Only three days later Audri was sitting on a wall with Simon and John, sharing an ale. Audri righted himself after falling from the wall into a pricking gorse bush. 'You pushed me on purpose' he whined at his friends. But they could only howl with laughter after watching him jump into the air like a frightened cat.

The weather was finer than it had been for weeks and although the cold was bitter, it felt good to spend time outdoors. It was approaching dusk and in the dim light he saw the shape of two figures furtively approaching the storehouse next to Maerwynn's house. He nudged Simon.

'Do you see that?'

Simon nodded. 'Looks like someone is trying to get in. Is that Maerwynn's?'

'No,' said John in a whisper. 'It belongs to old Matthew. The two houses used to belong to the same family.'

In unison, they dropped from the wall and crouched on the ground to be less likely to be seen in the darkness. One of the figures was fiddling with the door and a moment later it was flung open. The figure hesitated and looked around. Although for a second his eyes faced their direction, it seemed he couldn't make them out against the wall. He disappeared inside to be followed by his companion.

'That isn't right,' said Audri. 'They are robbing that store. Let's get them.'

He stood up and glanced at Simon and John.

'It isn't our problem,' said Simon. 'And they may be armed. We should fetch help.'

'From where?' said Audri. 'By the time we've summoned someone and explained, they'll be long gone and we may get the blame.'

John shrugged and got to his feet as did Simon. They followed Audri to the storehouse, walking as quietly as possible. The men inside made no attempt to be quiet, banging and clattering as they grabbed what they wanted. Audri slid inside the storehouse, followed by Simon and John. It took a moment for his eyes to adjust to the darkness and he gasped as he realised it was the messenger men stuffing cheeses into the sacks they carried.

Suddenly one of the men turned. 'Get out if you know what is good for you,' he snarled. 'We'll soon be gone.'

Audri stepped forward and tried to wrestle the sack out of the man's hand. The man kicked him to the ground. Simon moved forward to help him up but the man punched him in the face. John stood back, unsure what to do. Suddenly the door opened and Matthew appeared. He glanced around and started to shout. 'Robbers! I'm being robbed!'

The weasel man lunged forwards and grabbed Matthew. He drew a knife from his tunic and Audri heard a gurgle as Matthew's body dropped to the ground.

Audri jumped to his feet and moved towards the man, stopping when the man waved his knife at him. Suddenly, a group of men flung themselves through the door. 'What's wrong?' one shouted.

'Robbers! I have one of the robbers!' shouted one man.

Audri felt a blow to his head and the world went black as he fell to the ground.

Matthew was dead. The men dragged Audri, Simon and John outside, yelling at them as they pushed and pulled until they'd reached the manor house where they told

Lord Robert de Ayermin, that the boys needed to be locked up until the magistrate could attend.

Audri felt dizzy and unable to make sense of what was happening. When the magistrate arrived, he tried to explain but Simon and John were speaking at the same time. The magistrate shook his head and said they'd have enough time to explain to the court. He left and they decided to try and take a couple of hours sleep. But the moment they curled up on the floor, a man appeared and barked at them to follow him. He was carrying a large and heavy staff, which was enough to discourage any argument. A few minutes later they were huddled together in a stinking and cold stone room beneath the manor.

There was no more than ten feet in each direction. Damp coated the walls and a small pool of water in the far corner was spreading across the floor. The man who'd guided them left for a moment and returned with a bucket, which he tossed into the corner. There was no need to explain what that was for. Simon got to his feet and set it upright before dropping his breeches and pissing into it. He hadn't finished when the man slammed the door shut and they were suddenly wrapped in darkness.

Audri gasped. As his eyes adjusted, he became aware that a sliver of light entered the room from the narrow grill high up on the door, just enough so they could make out each other's bodies.

It was a long and miserable night. The single stone bench was no more comfortable than the floor, but it was at least dry. John grabbed a piece of straw from the floor and they drew lots for it. Audri won the draw and stretched along the bench while John and Simon lay huddled together on the floor. They lay sleeplessly and in silence until the light disappeared from the door. And then Audri drifted into a dreamless sleep.

The next morning, two men arrived and dragged the boys outside, saying they were being taken to town. Audri blinked hard as the light seared his eyes. He breathed deeply and looked up into the sky. It was filled with clouds but for now at least a gap allowed the sun its full power. More than that, the world now smelled sweet and a gentle breeze caressed his face, stroking him gently as if to tell him that all would be well. He almost smiled.

They tied the boys' hands and pushed them into a cart. The cart bounced and scraped along the ground as it made its way through the village. It was nearly halfway when Galeran appeared and stood in front of it and demanded to know what was happening.

'Stand clear, Galeran,' said one of the men. 'We're taking these murderers to town. They'll have their say at court.'

'My brother isn't a murderer! What's happened?'

Sensing Galeran wasn't going to move without an explanation, one of the men hurriedly gave an account.

'But what about the messenger men?' said Galeran.

'You're too quick to listen to your brother's fancies,' the man said. 'They haven't been near the village for days.'

Audri yelped in protest and one of the men slapped the back of his head. He groaned.

'We asked Father James when your brother told the magistrate it was them. He said they hadn't been to the village. More than that, he said they'd told him last week that they were taking a long trip up north to deliver a letter to the bishop. Your brother is trying to move the blame.'

'Galeran ...' Audri said plaintively. But it was of no use. The man talking to Galeran shoved him aside and the cart began to move again.

Galeran was yelling something but Audri couldn't make out what it was. Father James stood to one side, studiously observing their progress. Audri caught his eye and Father James smirked at him before turning and walking away.

The portmoot had only heard minor pleas of late – petty theft, an argument about land boundaries, a complaint that one woman had gossiped about another. A jury was swiftly chosen and the jurors immediately busied themselves, talking to everyone in the village so they might know the truth of the matter. They all knew Audri and his friends, having lived side by side with them for their whole lives. Many questions didn't need to be asked. And they didn't ask Galeran. There was no point in asking a brother to damn brother. They would already have known if Galeran and Audri had such a relationship. It was sad that Father James spoke so badly of Audri. His testimony weighed heavily.

Only two Mondays had to pass before the court was ready to hear the case.

Simon would be forever indebted to his uncle. He'd paid the jurors well enough to ensure that some denied having knowledge of Simon, despite having lived within a half mile of him for all their lives. Others stated that they were assured of his innocence. One, perhaps more generously paid than the rest, assured the court that Simon had been with him that night and so he couldn't have been responsible. It wasn't important. What mattered was that none of the jury was prepared to convict him.

John claimed benefit of clergy. True or not, if he could convince the court, he'd be able to walk free. Standing before the judge, he was handed a Bible and opened it reciting, '*Miserere mei, Deus, secundum misericordiam tuam ...*' It wasn't his destiny to meet with Death at this time.

Only Audri would meet the full wrath of the court. And they had more than enough to offer him.

The hearing was short, the decision already made.

The night before his death, Father James visited Audri. 'I don't wish to be shriven,' Audri said before Father James could open his mouth. 'Not by you.'

'Don't let your pride make you a fool,' the priest said loftily. He offered Audri a smirk before continuing. 'Confess your sins and accept the pain of your execution as reparation.'

'I have no sins to confess.'

Father James hissed. 'Everyone has sins to confess, you more than most. Confess your crime so you may speed your way to heaven. Earn yourself a good death.'

'I have no sins to confess,' Audri repeated. He turned away and faced the wall, waiting until Father James gave up and left.

Soon it grew dark and Audri curled up on the ground. He didn't sleep but lay still with his eyes closed, waiting for the dawn light to herald his death.

They came for him early. The man who opened the door refused to meet his eyes and simply reached out and pulled at Audri's arm to drag him outside the cell. There, he tied Audri's hands behind his back tightly, with a piece of stinking rope. It cut into the now festering wounds around his wrist. Audri allowed himself to be pulled and pushed as the man desired. Resisting would simply prolong things.

A small procession made its way to the gallows. Audri glanced to see if he recognised anyone. Some were his neighbours, others strangers. None of them spoke although one old woman he'd known since childhood wept as she walked at the head of the group.

Once Audri stood at the scaffold, silence fell as the hangman turned to him. 'Now,' he said. 'Now is your chance to make your peace with God. You may speak.'

Audri was expected to seek forgiveness, to forgive his executioner, to ask for the prayers of those staring at him. He knew what he was expected to say. He knew what they were waiting for. Instead he stood there, shaking like a beaten dog.

A minute later he dangled from on high. A gasp and he'd left this world, his glassy eyes lingered over the town square.

It wasn't yet over. Hanging alone was enough for a thief, but Audri's crimes required a more extensive punishment. Something that others could view and make them wonder if they would have the courage to meet their own deaths with fortitude.

A guard stepped forward and with a single blow, removed Audri's head. The small crowd gasped. Driven on by what seemed to be their excitement, but was in fact their agitation, he removed each limb. This wasn't so efficient. He had to hack and tear, becoming breathless from his efforts. But it didn't take long until he called for rope. The hangman leaned towards him with a length in his hand.

'You could have waited a while,' he said disapprovingly. 'Why the hurry?'

'Why not?' said the guard. He relished his job and tended to act like a child presented with a new plaything. The guard looked at the mess spread before him. Audri's tongue protruded between his lips and his face had grown dark, almost black. The guard shuddered. 'Henry!' he called out.

Immediately, another guard appeared at his side. The crowd hadn't moved but continued to watch with interest. The newly-arrived guard held a large basket. He helped to rope the pieces of Audri together and collected the bundle.

By the end of the day, the pieces of Audri were hanging in display on the old road that ran out of Marlborough and into Savernake Forest, as though his body parts were trying to make their way home. The birds were first to react to him. They wasted no time in feasting on his eyes and by the next morning only empty sockets gazed outwards. He was kept company by the skeleton of a man who'd killed his wife and child the previous year.

The next day Galeran stood on the road and stared at what remained of Audri, his flesh already blackened and shrunk. The damp in the air fed the putrid smell and Galeran gasped as he held a hand to his face. The wind whistled and the rain fell but Galeran didn't move. He stared until the sun sank below the horizon and he could see no more. He then turned to walk home.

Matilda waited as Galeran entered their house, unsure what to say. Galeran simply shook his head. They never mentioned Audri again.

CHAPTER 7

September 1316

'Go away,' said Finn.

The dog continued to yap at him and suddenly lunged forward and nipped Finn's ankle. It froze for a moment and turned to run, yelping as it disappeared into the distance.

It should have known better.

Apart from a sheep that stood regarding Finn with curiosity, there was no other living being to be seen. Indeed, the sheep hardly counted. It was a scrawny looking thing and had clearly lost its companions as it stood rigidly, waiting for someone to offer it directions. That someone wouldn't be Finn. He wasn't yet sure where he was heading, let alone in a position to offer guidance to another, even if that other was only a sheep.

The soggy ground tried to suck at Finn's feet every time he took a step to no avail. And it was slippery, slippery enough to make a normal man stumble and stagger unless they moved very slowly. But Finn glided over the top as if he were working with the earth rather than against it. The dim morning gloom did little to light his way, but he picked his path with ease.

He'd set off too early. It would be wise to sit and wait a while. As the church lay only a little way ahead, this was the obvious place to take his ease. It was an oddity that the church wasn't at the heart of the village but that did make it closer to the manor house on the hill. He squelched his way through the yard. A gentle push told him that the door was open, so Finn poked his head through.

The inside of the church looked sadly uncared for, covered in dust and grime. Nonetheless, it whispered a welcome to Finn. He reached into his memory and saw it as it used to be, how it had been before it was a church. This land had hosted a sacred building for centuries gone by and would do so for centuries to come. Things changed but only on the surface.

Finn stared. The painted scenes on the walls were grubby, and it was hard to make out what some people depicted were up to. They showed stories from the Bible – at least, that's what Finn assumed. There may have been other stories told alongside, but they were all stories so it mattered little. He paused and listened. It remained silent so he slid through the door, gently closing it. Then he walked past the font near the door and sat on the stone ledge against the wall.

Finn's eyes soon adjusted to the dim light and he managed to pick out the figures of the grotesques in the roof. Unless you already knew they were there, you'd be unlikely to notice them. But once you noticed them, they were hard to forget. The figure of a saint – his status shown clearly by the halo perched atop his head – seemed blissfully unaware of the demon behind him whose clawed fingers extended to grasp his throat. Another saint, in a similar predicament, had his mouth part open. Perhaps he could feel the breath of the demon behind him. Some years ago, Finn had heard a priest explain to a curious visitor that the demons were bent over due to the weight of the sins they carried. It didn't look that way to Finn; as far as he could see they were poised to attack. Especially that one with a wide smirk on its face and bulbous eyes.

Amongst the demonic figures were two women. One brandished long pointed claws and the other wore a winged headdress that looked as if it could carry her into the sky with little persuasion. And there was a tonsured cleric. How fitting he should loom over the man signifying goodness.

Finn smiled at the familiar figures. And he smiled yet more broadly as he made out the other grotesques of animals and monsters. And there, faded with time and buried among the other depictions, but not painted over, the head of a man who had hair and a beard made up of leaves. Vines sprouted from his mouth and nostrils, they were ladened heavily with fruit.

'Do you sleep now?' said Finn aloud to the face. 'Have you tired of your task? Is that why the rains won't stop falling and the crops are rotting in the fields?' He sighed. 'It has been too long, my friend.'

The door clattered open and Father James entered, stopping abruptly as he saw Finn. He gathered himself and walked into the church. Finn got to his feet.

'You are a traveller?' said the priest in a tone that implied to argue would be pointless. 'And you are here for morrow-mass? You're early.'

'No,' said Finn.

Father James looked confused. 'You believe you aren't early?'

'No, I'm not early. I hadn't intended to arrive at any specific time. No, I am not a traveller. I have lived only a little distance away for more summers than I can count. And no, I am not here for morrow-mass and—' Finn paused to cast a glance around the church '—it seems you must say it alone. I will take my leave.'

'There is much sickness and the hunger has rendered too many more fond of their sleep. If they don't wake, they won't hear the growl of their bellies,' the priest said defensively as if Finn were about to accuse him of being responsible for such a state of events.

Indeed, Finn briefly considered doing just that. Whether this priest was complicit in making the villagers' situation worse, he had no idea. But all priests carried a heavy load of guilt and that guilt was not always justified. It would be poor sport to indulge this topic further.

He ignored the still talking priest and made his way

to the church door. Outside, Finn turned to glance at the gargoyle above the door on the waterspout. This was of a man with his back turned and partly bent to display his bare arse to its fullest. His head twisted to face the view, his head split by a wide grin and protruding tongue. Finn briefly stuck his own tongue out at it before walking on. There was so much more written in the church than the priests acknowledged. So many old stories were told if you knew where to look.

It was now almost fully light. People would soon start appearing, going about their daily tasks. And the rain had ceased at last. He walked towards the green where a clutter of thatch-roofed houses huddled together in lines on either side, each with a garden surrounded by a fence, some with ducks and hens stabbing their beaks on the ground in the forlorn hope of finding grain.

Next to the well stood a blacksmith's workshop, house and a larger than usual house with three beehives in the garden. And next to the mill was a bakery. He would stop there first. Bakers always rose early, even when they had nothing to bake.

As Finn approached the bakery he saw a dumpy looking woman with flour in her hair, looking anxious as she inspected the contents of a sack.

'I have nothing baked at this hour,' she said in a wary tone as he approached. 'You will have to return later.'

'I am not here to buy bread.'

The woman looked at him in confusion. 'You will pay if you want bread,' she said determinedly.

'No,' said Finn. 'You misunderstand. I may return to buy bread but—'

'My husband will arrive in a few minutes,' responded the woman. The way she bit her lip revealed this to be a lie.

Finn simply nodded. 'I seek a bed for a few nights,' he said.

'There's no inn here,' the woman said. 'You'd do well to continue your walk into town. It won't take you more than an hour or so. That is more suited for travellers. Back the way you came.'

'I thank you, but I grow tired. Is there someone who takes in travellers?'

'Can you pay?'

Silently, Finn reached inside his tunic and retrieved his purse. He shook a few coins into his palm and showed the woman. She smiled approvingly. 'Such strange and old coins you have,' she mused. 'You could ask at the ale-house. She's been known to take people in – especially if you can offer a song or two.'

'I have a good voice,' said Finn.

The woman held her hand up as if he were about to burst into song. 'You don't need to convince me. There.' She pointed to the house opposite, on the other side of the green. 'You'll smell the brewing. Knock loudly. She's drunk as a thrush more often than not.'

Matilda was still yawning as she opened the door and surveyed the world. The unfamiliar voice had sparked her curiosity. 'Joan!' she called to the woman at the bakery. A plain and dumpy woman, Joan hid her sharp wit and eager eyes well. But not her sharp tongue. She'd once spread a tale that Galeran had paid a doxy at the market, saying she'd seen him pass her the coins with her own eyes. Matilda listened and indulged her story with pity and exasperation, not fully understanding the consequences of village gossip, especially from Joan. She later repeated the story to Galeran merely in passing rather than accusation. He'd looked at her grimly and left the house. When he returned, he'd said that Joan would not repeat that story. But that was long ago and there wasn't room for a grudge in such a small village.

Joan turned towards her and waved her over. 'You're out early,' she observed.

'I heard a stranger.'

'I saw him first,' said Joan with a huge grin spreading across her face. 'My William has been in the ground much longer than your Galeran and the nights grow ever colder.'

'It's getting warmer!' Matilda mused, raising an eyebrow.

'Not where it matters,' said Joan, sliding her hand down from her waist. 'Anyway, I know nothing about him but that he's seeking a bed for a few nights. I sent him to Agnes. She doesn't mind taking in travellers. And he said he can sing. You'll take an ale with me this evening so we can see if he's telling the truth?'

They took themselves to the pub that night but the stranger was not there, much to Matilda's disappointment.

With the mundanity of the village she would have welcomed tales from a stranger in town, but alas he was nowhere to be seen the entire night. The few locals that were there shared a drink with Matilda and filled her in on gossip she'd missed since not being out much these past few months. She felt a sudden sense of loss and realised she's missed Galeran more than she'd known. This led her to feel even worse for guilt for not realising this sooner.

'We thought you'd found your grave, we've barely seen you!' exclaimed Peter. Agnes immediately elbowed him hard in the stomach. He exclaimed in pain, but Matilda didn't mind, she wasn't easily offended any more. She shook her thoughts away and carried on with her ale.

CHAPTER 8

Winter 1315

Adelaide yawned all through Mass. Then she listened to Robert complain at length while they breakfasted. He complained about the weather, the fact that Howard – his reeve – was ill, that one of his horses was lame, and that the world simply refused to take the shape he wanted. So she yawned some more.

Robert glared at her. 'You could show a bit of interest,' he said.

'You're in an ill humour and it would make no difference,' Adelaide responded absently. She picked up another piece of bread and inspected it closely.

For a brief second, Robert glared at her again and shrugged. 'I need to go over the accounts with Howard this morning,' he said. 'And there's a dispute about grazing he wants to explain to me. It can probably be answered by simply saying "no" but he'll want to make it sound more important.'

'I thought you said he was ill.'

'Not so ill that he can't speak with me. He's just refusing to ride anywhere.'

Someone was bustling around and clearing away the remains of breakfast. Adelaide grabbed her wine before that got cleared away too. Every time she put anything down, someone moved it. It was completely maddening. She had nowhere to relax or hide, even in her own room. There always needed to be a body attending to her when she washed and dressed.

Robert got to his feet and stretched. 'You do look tired,' he observed. A smile crept across his face. 'Do you think that you are…'

'No,' Adelaide said firmly. 'I am not. Not yet, sir.'

After opening his mouth and closing it again without uttering a sound, Robert left the room. Adelaide waited and nothing happened so she coughed loudly. A moment later, Emma appeared, her hair sticking up in all directions as if she'd only woken a few moments ago. Perhaps she had. 'She's here,' Emma said.

'Who is?' Adelaide asked. Emma's habit of beginning conversations halfway through was extremely annoying.

'The girl I got to help with the laundry. Do you want to speak to her?'

To talk to *anyone* would break the monotony. 'Bring her in,' said Adelaide.

While waiting for Emma to return, Adelaide picked up her sewing basket. The section of tapestry she was working on was very dull, being a repetitive section of birds in the background, but the faster she completed it, the sooner she would be able to work on the more interesting – no, it was all dull. But she would work on it because that is what mornings were for.

It had been twelve weeks since she had married Lord Robert. This was a very different life. With her father dying while she was so young, her mother had left Adelaide and her three sisters to their own devices. Their nurse hadn't worried about what they did as long as no one was injured and no one complained. So the girls rode for miles, played music and ordered masters to visit so they could study whatever grabbed their interest. They'd known, of course, that such a life couldn't last and they would have to marry but that day came much sooner than Adelaide had hoped.

It might have been worse. Lord Robert de Ayermin owned a sizable manor and things appeared to run smoothly there. He looked pleasant, could read and write and hadn't sired any children in the village – at least, to her knowledge.

Nyle. She should have been married to Nyle. But Nyle was dead.

Adelaide shivered.

When Robert had first sent a message to her mother and arrived at their home with his full retinue, Adelaide's mother had been so in awe of him that she'd been ready to agree to anything he asked. They'd sat together drinking her good wine until the girls returned from that day's adventures, chatting loudly. And when Adelaide's mother presented her daughters, his eyes were on Adelaide. He'd come seeking a wife, her mother had said all of a hurry. A wife from a good family. He had been betrothed but his intended had taken the veil. So he was seeking a wife.

Not me, Adelaide had thought. How easy it was to be wrong.

Her sister Maboly fluttered her eyelashes at the lord, but he looked away. He glanced at Isobel and Alaine but their mother flapped her hands and said they were too young – unless he had in mind a long betrothal? Adelaide? Oh, no. She was promised.

Robert gave a small tight smile and took his leave.

He returned a week later and Adelaide hid in the barn as soon as she saw him approach. Her mother was angry, saying they couldn't afford to upset him. Another week went by and he arrived while Adelaide was taking a lesson on her flute. She laid the instrument down when he arrived and said she needed her bed as there was a pain in her head that wouldn't cease. Her mother wrung her hands and cursed herself and their father for raising such wilful children.

A week after that, Nyle was found dead. He lay in a ditch, his head caved in. No one knew what had happened. No strangers had been nearby – except Robert's man. Such a large man couldn't hide himself easily. But he'd said he was simply carrying a message for his master. Perhaps he was.

That was six months ago. Arrangements had been made without Adelaide's knowledge while she walked through the woods, her heart aching and her head filled with a fog. When she pleaded with her mother, her mother wept and said she didn't know what else to do. Adelaide needed to be married and who else was there? How could they refuse a man like Lord Robert? And when Adelaide was married, he would send some men to help work her mother's land and to repair their house, something sorely needed. He would ensure that Adelaide's mother needn't worry about how she would live out her twilight years. *Did Adelaide not care for her mother? Such a selfish daughter.*

The wedding had been pleasant enough. Maboly had thrown her arms around Adelaide when it was over and whispered that if she sent a message, she would bring a horse and take her where she wished. They could ride away together; Adelaide need only ask. Adelaide had gently pushed her away and said that the world was not like that.

All she thought of that day was Nyle and when she said 'I do' her heart withered.

Emma flung the door open and ushered a young woman into the room. She held her head down in respect so Adelaide had to peer carefully to see her face. She was pretty in an ordinary way with reddish-brown hair and hazel eyes that sparked with intelligence.

Emma elbowed the woman and she bobbed and said, 'M'lady.'

Adelaide nodded in response and looked at Emma for help.

'She's come to help with the laundry,' said Emma smugly. 'Her name's Matilda.' Because Adelaide had clearly forgotten, she added, 'You expressed an interest in meeting her.'

Had she? Probably. At some point Lord Robert had said it would be useful if she became familiar with everyone who worked at the manor in case he wasn't present or was ill and she needed to make decisions. Although in reality the reeve would surely attend to such matters. But she still didn't know what to say.

Adelaide's flaxen hair reminded Matilda of ash from a waning fire and thought how frail she seemed. Almost as though her essence had left her.

'There is much laundry to do this week,' Adelaide attempted, although she had no idea if that was the case.

Matilda nodded and offered a weak smile. 'You can be sure it will be done,' she said in a tone that brooked no argument.

'Very well,' said Adelaide.

Silence fell as they waited for Adelaide to add something. 'Do you like being a laundress?' she asked wildly. Emma looked at her as if she'd gone mad.

Matilda raised her eyebrows. 'I'm not a laundress – although my mother was. Emma said you needed help because someone was sick so ...'

'There's sickness here?' Adelaide asked Emma.

Emma rolled her eyes and Adelaide tried to look crossly at her. It would make no difference. 'Bess fell down,' Emma said crisply. 'She'll be well but her ankle stops her from standing for long. You can't do laundry if you need to sit all the while. I *told* you.'

She probably had. Adelaide's ears closed in protest whenever Emma began to speak. Then she caught Matilda's eye and realised she was struggling to hold back a smile. She looked so like Maboly, and at that moment Adelaide ached for her sister's company.

Emma bobbed and indicated Matilda should do the same. She ushered her out of the door and Adelaide was alone again – briefly. No doubt one of her ladies would soon arrive and express joy at the quality of her embroidery as they did every morning. The thought made her shudder. She flung the door open and called, 'Emma! Come back. And bring the girl.'

Within seconds Emma and Matilda were standing in front of her looking confused. 'Do you have a neat sewing hand?' Adelaide asked Matilda.

'I do,' said Matilda proudly. 'A very neat hand and I can sew speedily.'

'Then you can help me with my tapestry,' Adelaide said decisively. 'That will be all, Emma.'

Emma bobbed half-heartedly and left the room.

Adelaide sighed. Then she reached into her sewing basket. Buried deeply within it was a small book. Adelaide pulled it out and sat on the bench by the window, the rain patted down against the dull panes that held the warmth of the fire inside. She gestured to the basket. 'It needs birds,' she said.

'Then it shall have birds,' Matilda said as she pulled out the cloth and threads and sat on a low stool a few feet away from Adelaide. She threaded a needle and after giving the tapestry little more than a cursory glance, she began to sew.

'Tell me if you hear anyone coming,' said Adelaide. And she began to read.

CHAPTER 9

September 1316

Planting had been almost impossible with the rains washing everything away, and the few crops they'd managed to put into the ground were hard to harvest because of flooding. Everything was covered in a coat of fuzzy mildew and mould. And still the rain continued to fall, although it was little more than a light drizzle today. Please God the weather gets better soon. If the autumn harvest was like last year's, the villagers would need to eat each other.

The fog hung over the ground like a sodden blanket. It would be no use to go into it today. Matilda coughed. Immediately, she panicked and imagined sinking into illness and dying within the week. She shook herself. Of course she'd coughed. She'd been outdoors for three hours now, scrabbling and looking for something to eat. And she hadn't drunk anything since rising that morning. If she didn't take care, she'd imagine her life away. Rubbing her back, she straightened up and surveyed the garden.

Maybe a few beans would grow. Maybe. She tied her loose red plait then threw the braid over her shoulder, and poked half-heartedly at the soil again wondering if a mushroom or two lay beneath a stone.

She hadn't asked what the meat was that Roger had brought round last week, but he hadn't mentioned his dog for some time.

The hunger now brought with it a sort of madness and corrupted the blood. Matilda had watched in horror as Simon had slowly lost the ability to walk due to the spasms attacking his body. He was confined to his bed before long, and she sat with him when his mother needed to work the fields. Simon's mind had soon departed and he screamed at the monsters that were only in his head. His fingers began to darken until they turned black, and one by one, fell off. His toes were likely the same but he raved too hard for Matilda to take a look. Thankfully, he left the world before his arms were completely gone too. His mother wept but Matilda guessed she wept as much from relief as from sorrow.

The madness had frightened Simon's family so much that they'd left in the dead of night. Others followed them over the next few days. Good. Fewer bellies to feed.

But for every person who left, two or three strangers would arrive in the hope that this village would offer more than the one they'd left. Sometimes they stayed a night or two, sometimes moved on immediately after seeing the expressions their demand for bread brought to people's faces. They would work, they insisted, and work hard. But there was no work to be had. Anyone begging didn't last for long.

One or two had food to sell. That cost dear but you can't eat coins. Matilda had a few coins. She'd sold Galeran's tools only two weeks before – and his good hat. She'd wanted to keep it for the memory, but memories alone wouldn't keep her alive. Maerwynn had persuaded her to accept payment for helping with the sick.

'They make profit from the fields because of your help,' she'd said. 'There's no shame in letting them pay for it.' Although accepting money from the sick and dying felt wrong to Matilda, she accepted the money; what choice did she have?

She'd bought a hen but there'd been no eggs for days now. Perhaps it was past its time. Matilda had kept it firmly shut up indoors. In these times, it would fast disappear if she left it to its own devices outside.

Her eyes widened as she spotted something in the dirt. One pod. One peapod – yellowing and tight with the succulent beans within. She couldn't wait. Saliva filled her mouth as she carefully removed it from the stalk and examined it. Ripe and ready to eat. It wasn't worth boiling water for such a small meal.

Carefully, she popped the pod open and slid the bean into her mouth. *Oh!*

All too soon it was finished. She scraped among the dirt, hoping against sense that she'd missed another pod, that some – one – had survived and waited for her to find it. But she knew in truth that there'd be none.

Out of the corner of her eye Matilda caught a glimpse of a fox – or was it a dog? She jumped up and span around to shoo it away, then yelped at the sight of the man looking smilingly down at her. It was the man she'd seen talking to Joan. She jumped to her feet to find herself greeted by a broad smile.

'Finn,' he said. 'That's what they call me. And you are Mistress Matilda?' He held her gaze for some time, seemingly unable to look away.

Matilda nodded calmly, brushing some sweat and hair from her face with a mud-stained hand.

'The churchyard,' he said.

Matilda looked at him, baffled.

'Some chickweed grows behind the wall. I saw it yesterday but I don't think anyone else has noticed it. It tastes good.'

'Show me.' Her voice quivered, this was no time for pride. She felt a bubble of excitement pop inside her stomach, but this was soon replaced with the hungry promise of food, even if it was from a stranger. She'd had many a warning as a girl from her mother not to talk alone with men, much less go off with them. But as she lived alone in her house day by day she felt something growing inside her; a boldness that was liberating.

Finn nodded and turned to walk towards the church with Matilda at his side. She saw Joan wave from her garden as she watched them pass, her face betraying malicious curiosity. Matilda smiled inwardly. Joan had always been good at being in other people's business so everyone tried to tell her as little as possible. She filled in the gaps with fancies that entertained them but no one believed. Before she returned, Matilda would no doubt have married the stranger and borne him three children.

Matilda didn't care, it felt good to have a man at her side. Since Galeran had gone, she'd missed a warm body next to hers. They walked in silence and once they reached the churchyard, Finn stepped smartly to the left and leaned over the old stone wall. Matilda imitated him. There, sheltered from the wind and rain, a patch of ground was covered in chickweed. She attempted to climb over the wall but the slick surface made it impossible for her to grip onto it and she slid to the ground.

'Let me,' said Finn.

Matilda was about to protest and then realised only pride was prompting her to do so, and this man intrigued her, so she bit her tongue. She allowed Finn to lift her and hoist her onto the other side of the wall. A small thrill passed through her at his touch. She watched as he climbed over it, effortlessly.

Without saying a word, she bent down and grabbed the bunches of chickweed, shoving them into her mouth.

'There's more,' said Finn. 'And I've seen some mallow.'

Matilda nodded and followed him as he walked a little further on. There, in another place of shelter grew mallow, as he'd promised. Matilda bent down and gathered as much as she could bundle into her apron. 'There is something special about this land,' she said softly. 'But we must leave some to flower, we shouldn't take it all.'

Finn smiled a huge grin and shook his head a little 'I think if I'd shown anyone else this, they would have taken as much as they could carry and left none to flower.'

'Not everyone would,' Matilda interrupted with a shrug … 'just most of them,' she laughed.

'So will you show anyone else this place?' Finn tested.

'Perhaps. it depends on how hungry I get,' she laughed again. Her smile turning to a bitter thought, she imagined herself coming back to this spot in the cover of darkness to raid the area.

Reluctantly, she got to her feet. She struggled not to empty the contents of her apron into her mouth now, but she needed to keep some back until later. 'I must return,' she said, although she had no idea what she was returning for. An empty house.

Finn nodded and his expression changed to one of concern as Matilda swayed where she stood. 'You need to sit a while,' he said. He cast his eyes over the churchyard. 'There's little that's dry,' he said. 'Maybe we can sit on the step.'

The air was eerily silent. Certainly, there was no sound to suggest that the priest might arrive any time soon. With three villages to tend to, sometimes days would go by before he appeared. Matilda strode over to the step and sat as far to the end as she could, allowing space for Finn to sit next to her without touching. And then it occurred to her. He hadn't arrived at her garden to show her chickweed.

'You were looking for me?' she asked all of a sudden. 'You sought me for a reason?'

'I did, but your need to eat seemed more urgent.'

The kindness in his voice sounded of genuine concern. 'Why did you seek me?' Matilda persisted. And she coughed again. She still hadn't had a drink.

'Joan mentioned you were good with a needle.' Finn said. 'I have a tear in my tunic.' He indicated the side of his tunic which was starting to gape open. A fresh and clean tear that looked as if he'd made it with his own hand.

'I can repair that easily,' said Matilda, inspecting it more closely. 'And that will repay you for showing me the herbs.'

'Oh I insist on paying you for your work,' Finn pressed. 'I merely took you for a stroll, the ground gave you a gift, not I,' he continued.

'Well, I also insist. Shall we return? I'll do it now.'

Finn stood up and held out his hand to help Matilda to her feet. 'That would be very kind of you,' he said with a brief deep bow accepting his loss of the battle.

'And you will take an ale with me?' A statement more than a question.

'It would be my delight,' said Finn gravely.

Matilda grabbed Finn's hand and a shock travelled throughout her body. Immediately, she dropped his hand. As she stepped away from him for a brief moment, she fancied she saw a wolf stand high on its legs and loom towards her. She gasped and turned to look at Finn. He was smoothing down the front of his tunic.

She really needed that ale.

71

When she awoke the next morning the world sounded different. It *felt* different, but Matilda couldn't put her finger on why. Then she realised – it wasn't raining. She pulled back the shutter and in disbelief, she looked into the sky. There were thick clouds above, but they were wispy and white rather than bulbous and grey. And the sun shone weakly, but it was shining, it wasn't hidden.

In fear that any delay would cause the skies to burst open, Matilda hurriedly dressed. She could have sworn that Thom smiled at her when she unfastened his rope. 'A foolish moment,' she said in a low voice to him. 'But it's good to feel foolish sometimes.'

And before she had time to think about what she was doing, she was on Thom's back and coaxing him down the path. It had been so long since she had ridden for the joy of it. She let Thom set the pace and once he realised, he began to speed up. They made their way through the village and past the church – she hadn't been so far in weeks. Then Thom veered sharply to the left and Matilda gasped. He was taking her to the river. They had to pass through the woods but the trees were sparse here, and without so many fallen leaves to make the ground bounce, Thom was able to march on confidently. As if to reinforce this, he gave a whinny and Matilda patted him briefly.

The river was now in sight. It was narrow and deceptively deep. Probably much deeper than in the past – it looked wider too, but perhaps her mind was playing tricks. Matilda coaxed Thom to a stop and jumped down. It could be dangerous if they got too close. In parts, the banks were steep and the sodden earth could collapse without warning. She took a deep breath. The air tasted sweeter here, cleaner as if the river gave it life. Thom suddenly dipped his head and began to munch at a patch of grass so she dropped the rope and walked a few feet closer to the river's edge.

That's when she saw him. At first, she wasn't sure if she had seen anything at all, but there was definitely someone swimming. Matilda shaded her eyes and squinted, she pulled a tendril of red hair back over her ear. A head bobbed up and down, arms ploughed rhythmically through the water as the figure smoothly made its way downriver and then turned back and swam directly towards her. It wasn't until it was only a few yards away that she realised it was Finn.

He raised a hand in salute and she waited for him to climb out of the river and join her but he turned again and swam back in the direction he'd come from. He looked as if he was part of the river, as if he made his home there. There were tales of creatures who lived in the water and only emerged to be amongst people for a short time. If such creatures existed, Finn could have been one of them.

She waited a little longer but he didn't return.

It began to rain and she made her way home, a little disappointed but exhilarated with the sight of Finn and her ride with Thom.

CHAPTER 10

March 1316

Matilda snapped out of her dream and wondered why she still toiled in the field. Nothing she did was of any value. Everything in the ground smelled rotten and was frozen hard. With each step her cracked leather boots released a foul stench of decay from the muddied ground, forcing her to wheeze as it filled her nostrils.

Each day was the same. Night brought the blessing of oblivion, some time away from the monster of loneliness and hunger, gnawing from within, demanding to be fed. But the monster awoke with the light of dawn. And it was so much worse with Galeran being away. The nights were longer and colder, and it took Matilda much longer to fall asleep.

She hadn't wanted him to go. In fact, she'd pleaded with him not to leave her alone. Together they would be stronger, she'd insisted. But Galeran was stubborn and the more she pleaded, the more he insisted.

'I'll find work,' he'd said confidently. 'So many people

are on the move that someone will have been let down. They'll want a man to come in for a day or two to work their land or help with the animals.'

'There aren't so many cattle left now,' Matilda pointed out.

'But there are more alive than dead. And those that remain need good care. Someone might need help building a shelter or digging or clearing some land. I can do that. And once I have money, I'll buy whatever I can and we'll eat well, for a time, at least,' he insisted through a worried smile.

He'd been gone for over a week.

Matilda stared blankly at the fingers of mud that crawled across her shoes. They came to life and, like some strange and ancient beast, they slithered slowly across her foot. As she watched, they edged upward. *They are claiming me for the soil. They will drag me into the ground to rot.*

Matilda's heart beat faster and faster as panic began to take a hold of her. *I will be lost in the earth!* She opened her mouth to let out a low scream but hadn't the strength to produce more than a croaky squeak. She tried again but the urge to scream had gone.

There was a sound in the distance. Was it her name? She strained to hear and looked to see where the noise was coming from. She would have stepped forward towards the sound, but the fingers held her, tightening their grip and preventing her from moving. Staring down, she saw the sad yellowing leaves of the cabbages. There were no edges, nothing to mark where the leaves ended and the earth began. They were becoming one. And they stank.

The earth pulled so hard. She fell to her knees, her cracked and bleeding hands plunged into the ice that had formed in ploughed divots. She felt herself being dragged down, down, down. Her panic turned into blind terror. She forced her eyes open wide and took short heaving breaths through gritted teeth. *It is but a dream. It is but a dream!* she insisted to herself as a teenager tries to reassure themselves after waking from a childish nightmare.

A dream? This beast, whatever it was, had meant to eat her. She tipped forward and sank into the cold wet sludge until she was submerged to her thighs, her hips. There was a pull as it oozed over her stomach. She wanted to scream but was too scared to open her mouth lest the mud fill her throat. She was sinking. *Perhaps it's better not to fight. I can welcome the release of death and the peace it will bring.*

'Matilda!' The voice sounded far, far away. Too far away to help her.

'Matilda!' And again. But this time the shout pierced the fog with some strength. It was the shout of someone living. The voice of someone from this world and not the next. It was a familiar voice. She lifted her head and turned to look.

Roger was at the door of her house and he was calling her name, again and again.

And now he was banging hard at the door. Matilda

looked down at her hands. They felt as if they were no longer part of her body. They were so cold that she couldn't move them. Any attempt to wriggle her fingers only resulted in pain shooting up her arm. The earth would take her, it would take her soon and then she could rest.

But nothing was pulling at her; she was free to move. Matilda weakly forced herself to stand up. Her skirts were soaked with heavy mud and rotting leaves. They weighed heavily on her body and made strange wet sounds as she pulled them more tightly around herself so she might walk across the field. She needed to find out what Roger wanted. Her skirts like an echo of the dream, dragged at her, trying to draw her back into the field. *No! Enough of this foolishness, 'tis just the hunger in my belly and the pain in my head!*

Every step was a battle against the mud. But it was a small battle compared to others she had fought lately. The field was of no use to anyone. There was nothing to eat there. There was nothing to eat anywhere. There was going to be nothing to eat for a longer time to come and everyone knew it.

'Matilda!' Roger called again. He turned and looked in her direction. But the fog hung too thick for him to be able to see her properly until she was only an arm's breadth from him. 'Roger?' she said as she tapped his shoulder. 'What ails you?'

Roger started. 'Matilda! I have been calling and calling you.'

'And now I am here. I was in the field... I hoped...'

There was no need to finish. Roger would know what she hoped. The whole country shared the same hope.

'I am so sorry,' began Roger, Matilda's blood ran cold. 'It's Galeran, he… Why are you covered in mud?'

'I fell,' said Matilda shortly. 'But what of Galeran? Where is he?'

'I found him. He collapsed on the road between our house and here. I assume he was on his way home?'

She glanced up and realised the sun had indeed sunk low in the sky. *Surely it wasn't so late?* She couldn't have been in the field for so long.

'Where is he?' she repeated.

Roger made an odd stuttering noise and gestured a bundle of cloth and firewood in his cart. Sharp pointed sticks jutting out against the bag containing them. Although, on further inspection, they weren't sticks, it was Galeran. It wasn't kindling, those were his bones. He had no flesh on his body to surround them. And he didn't move. She leaned forward. He smelled of death. In only fourteen nights, Death had laid his hands on Galeran.

Matilda felt nauseated despite her concern. But there was nothing in her belly to depart it. She stifled a dry retch that threatened to turn into a sob.

'I had to bring him in my cart,' said Roger. 'I couldn't carry him alone and there was no one nearby to help. I didn't want to leave him on the road. He might not have survived.'

'Thank you, Roger,' Matilda said, noticing the tears that threatened to drip down his face. 'Thank you for bringing him home. God knows how long he would have lain there if you hadn't.'

'We need to get him indoors,' Roger responded. 'And try to warm him.'

The two of them pulled at Galeran and wrestled him out of the cart. Holding him upright, they pulled him into the house. Other than letting out a low groan when his head hit the doorpost while Matilda was struggling to keep a hold of him and open the door at the same time, Galeran didn't utter a sound.

Once they were inside, they lay Galeran in front of the fire. It was nearly completely out but Matilda grabbed the small pile of kindling at the side and looked at it doubtfully.

'Burn it,' said Roger. 'Galeran needs to be warm. I will find you more kindling.' When Matilda didn't respond, he grabbed the kindling from her and worked on getting the fire alight. Matilda reached for the bedding and propped Galeran's head up before wrapping him in blankets. Somehow, it felt even colder inside than it had outdoors. She pulled her shawl tighter around herself and huddled next to Galeran, close to the fire. Matilda reached for Galeran's hand and began to stroke it absently.

'I tried to find more wood,' implored Matilda. 'But it was too wet to bring indoors. I did look.' She had. She'd wandered for hours despairingly and returned with nothing that wouldn't take weeks in a store to dry.

Roger looked at her sympathetically. 'I know you did,' he said. 'Do you have something he can drink?'

'Nought but water.'

Roger grimaced. 'He needs milk. Something to build his strength. Even ale would be better than water.'

'We have no more ale.' Matilda's mouth watered at the thought of milk. It had been too long since she'd tasted it.

'And do you have anything to eat?' Roger asked gently. 'An egg? Don't you have chickens?' He looked around the house. It was definitely empty of chickens. Matilda missed them. They brought warmth and a happy sound as they clucked their way around the house, even though she'd grumbled when they threatened to trip her, they were a part of the home.

Matilda stared at Galeran. 'No. They were taken by the bastard fox a week past. There's no bread. Just a few beans I can boil. We'd hope to buy something. But the weather has stopped us going to town and there's nothing in the village. Maerwynn gave me two eggs three days ago but she can't afford to give us more.' She sighed. 'I think it's the Lord's will to punish us.'

'Punish you for what?' Roger said in a frustrated tone.

'Galeran and his brother never understood when to keep their silence.' Matilda poked at the fire. It was a little warmer.

'Let's put him into bed,' said Roger. 'And I'll go and find something he can eat. Maerwynn will likely spare another egg when I tell her how sick Galeran looks. And I have some ale left at home.'

Matilda nodded and watched blankly as Roger hauled Galeran into bed. Then he shook his head and left.

CHAPTER 11

September 1316

Four years they'd been together; she'd bought him with her first earned money when he was a year old. It was a fortunate purchase. When the man had led the horses into the village and called for buyers, one glance was all it took for Matilda to decide she needed to own him more than anything. It had taken every penny she had. Maerwynn had told her later that she shouldn't have looked so eager, she should have beaten the man down in price, but Matilda had been too scared that he would shrug and move on if she didn't seal the deal immediately.

And when Maerwynn had seen how sweet and gentle Thom was, and how strong when pulling his cart, she'd admitted that Matilda had made the right decision. His front legs set wide apart, huge chest and hindquarters made him the perfect horse for his job. He carried his loads without complaint as if he'd been placed on this earth for exactly that purpose.

At least, he'd never complained before today. He'd

stared at the sparse and soggy grass as Matilda had been poking at the soil in the hope that something edible had crept in and grown while she hadn't been looking. She was waiting for him to eat so she could take him out to work on the field. Nothing was growing, but nothing would grow unless she spent some time clearing the soaked and rotting leaves and stalks that currently coated it. But when she'd wheeled the cart over to Thom he'd made an odd noise and backed away.

Matilda cooed in encouragement. 'Stay still, Thom,' she admonished him as she struggled to attach him to the cart.

Thom gave her a withering look and slowly but firmly backed away.

'Thom!' She grabbed at his reins and pulled. Thom opened his eyes wide and pulled back, but half-heartedly as if he knew he would have to do what Matilda wanted but intended to make it as difficult as possible.

She couldn't afford to waste time like this. The rain was lighter than it had been for days but it could soon start falling heavily. Matilda patted Thom on his nose. 'Good boy. It's time to go.' She gave him a brief tug.

Thom stared at her and refused to move.

'It seems he doesn't want to work today,' Finn observed.

Matilda jumped. *Where had he come from?* She smiled in welcome. 'It isn't his decision.' Although it would do no good at all, she tugged at Thom again. He ignored her and instead gave Finn an imploring look.

'You don't tie him up at night?' Finn said. 'Everyone else does; aren't you afraid he'll wander off?'

'Not particularly. He won't go. We love each other too much,' she sighed.

'No, I need him and he needs me,' she said more to herself than to Finn or Thom.

Finn leaned against the fence with his arms folded. 'Do you need some help?' he asked.

Matilda shrugged. 'Unless you have an apple or two hidden on your person, I don't see how you can help.'

'If I had two apples, you and I would be eating them now, Matilda,' said Finn. 'You know that don't you, boy?' he added sternly in Thom's direction.

Thom tipped his head towards Finn in interest and Matilda smiled. 'I think he likes you, but all he heard was "apple".'

'Apple,' repeated Finn and Thom responded with a short neigh.

'Don't promise him what you can't give,' admonished Matilda.

'No, you're right. But I can make a different promise.' Finn walked over and patted Thom and leaned forward and whispered in his ear. Thom nuzzled Finn.

'He does like you!'

Finn whispered again in Thom's ear and then so fast that Matilda could hardly believe it was happening, he attached Thom to the cart and began to lead him out of the garden. Thom happily strolled alongside Finn, who seemed to walk in the mud with such ease. 'Where do you want to take him?' Finn called back over his shoulder.

'To the field along that way,' Matilda said pointing as she rushed to join Finn. 'I need to clear the ground.'

Finn nodded and they walked companionably to the field.

Matilda was covered in mud and ached all over when she returned but she'd achieved what she'd planned and more. Thom had willingly done all she asked, seeming to read her mind and pulling the cart in the direction she wanted as soon as she decided what to do next. There was more work to be done, but now the rain was heavier, it was enough for today. Joan called out a greeting as she approached her house.

'I see you've been talking to the stranger,' she said when Matilda walked over to exchange a few words. 'He's wasted no time getting his feet under your table, has he?' She raised her eyebrows meaningfully.

'He's good with Thom,' Matilda said.

'Just Thom?' Joan asked with a raised eyebrow. 'He was at your house yesterday as well.'

'He helped me gather some firewood,' said Matilda in irritation. *Is she watching me?*

'Not my concern,' said Joan in a tone that implied anything that happened in the village was her concern. She looked closely at Matilda. 'You look hearty enough. So you managed to escape the pestilence Galeran carried?

That was good fortune. Will you come to take an ale with me this evening? I haven't exchanged a word with anyone but the chickens these last three days and Agnes said we should go to her house.'

Matilda couldn't think of a reason to refuse even though she'd have been happy to spend another evening alone, dreaming of life as it used to be. Although she might not have been alone for long. Maerwynn called every couple of days and Roger stopped by most days. And Finn somehow had a reason to knock on her door at least once a day. She'd begun to look forward to his visits. 'Why not,' she said. 'I'll bury the rubbish from the cart and clean this mud off me and then come to find you.'

'I won't be hard to find,' said Joan as she turned away.

It was almost two hours before Matilda felt ready to relax. The moment she tapped on Joan's door, it was flung open and before she could say a word, Joan propelled her down the path and towards Agnes's house. 'You took forever!' she complained.

Agnes beamed when she opened her door revealing her broken and blackened teeth. 'You came! Joan said she would ask you but I worried you were grieving too strongly to want to drink with us.'

Matilda immediately felt guilty. Although she obviously missed Galeran, she'd thought about him less and less as each day went by. Her fear of being alone had been misplaced – she barely had a moment to herself. Truth be told, she enjoyed time alone, coming and going when she pleased, not having to be beholden to another's whims and desires. She'd never had it before; it was freeing. But it was better not to risk disapproval by allowing others to see her enjoy her own company. And sometimes her body craved the touch of another.

Despite not being too proud to accept help when it was offered, she rarely had to ask for it – only when a task required two bodies. 'No, not at all,' she said. 'It will be good to spend some time with friends.' She barely knew Agnes – she was friendly with Joan but Matilda had never done more than exchange a few polite words with her, mainly because Galeran had never liked her, saying she was too much of a gossip for his taste. But Matilda reasoned that Agnes had never done any harm to her.

'Can we come inside?' Joan asked briskly.

Agnes stepped aside and they entered. Finn was sitting by the fire next to Agnes's husband, Godfrey. Peter, the local blacksmith, was also there, sitting on a low stool at the table and studying a piece of paper with a frown on his face. They looked up and offered greetings. Not so long ago, the room would have been filled with people and laughter. It looked sadly empty.

Matilda and Joan sat on the floor with the others and instantly a cup of ale was pushed into Matilda's hand. 'Drink well,' said Agnes. 'I have made a new batch and we have plenty.'

Matilda needed no further persuasion. After her third cup, she decided that she never wanted to move again. She couldn't help but glance over at Finn, even when silence befell the room. She often caught his eye as if he'd been staring first. She felt a welling of excitement when her eye caught his. They were the most beautiful amber, which shone against his black hair. Lights to become lost in. He could never seem to look away first; how long would he hold her gaze if she let him?

They'd all chatted happily about how they'd spent the last few days and Godfrey told them a long involved tale about how the chickens had escaped from their pen a few days ago and had been found after many hours searching walking determinedly along the road to town. Matilda laughed until the tears fell from her eyes. And Peter told a tale about when he was a child and had fallen in the river because he thought he was being chased by a monster. 'It was no more than a fox,' he said finally. 'But I thought it was as big as a man and it spoke to me.'

'What did it say?' asked Matilda in fascination.

Joan snorted. Ignoring her, Peter said, 'It told me to take care of my mother. That she had little time left for this world and that I should go home.' He looked thoughtfully at the fire. 'She died five days later.'

Matilda shuddered and a silence fell on the room.

'You must have a tale or two,' said Joan to Finn. 'We know little about you and your tales will be new to us.'

Finn smiled. 'I am no good at telling tales, but I could offer a song?'

'A song now, and perhaps a tale later,' Joan said insistently.

Finn got to his feet and cleared his throat. Then he began to sing. It was a strange and unfamiliar air that spoke of ages past. And he had the voice of an angel.

There was never, ever one but she;
The memory makes my soul dance free.
Spring blossoms with birdsong,
The nightingale calls.
Summer's nights are long,
Fading to Harvest.
Winter winds are strong,
As the trees shed.

I sigh, I mourn.
I wish I'd ne'er been born.
There was never, ever one but she.

Like the others, Matilda froze and let her mouth drop open in astonishment, a warm and strangely familiar sentiment swelled in her stomach. Once Finn had finished, he dropped back down to the floor.

Joan elbowed him. 'You sing like that and expect only to give us one song? Again.'

Finn grinned at her, got to his feet again and gave them a deep bow. And he sang again.

'Enough,' he said holding his hand up when Joan opened her mouth. 'Enough for now.'

'I could play my flute a while,' said Peter.

'And I my lute,' added Godfrey. 'And we can all sing.'

As soon as Godfrey and Peter started playing the old tunes they'd grown up with, they all sang along – except Finn. He joined in from time to time but often demurred saying this song or another wasn't known to him. Agnes produced more and more ale and when Joan got to her feet saying the hour was late, Matilda stood with her and the room spun.

Agnes laughed. 'You look as if you need your bed,' she observed.

'Let me walk you back,' said Finn, jumping to his feet.

Joan shook her head and they'd left before Matilda could blink. 'I would be in your debt,' she said to Finn.

'Go,' said Agnes. 'We will do this again soon.'

'Thank you,' mumbled Matilda as Finn took hold of her arm and gently guided her out of the door.

The world swayed as Matilda stepped carefully along the path. Finn kept a tight hold of her elbow and they set off on the short walk back.

'You come from nowhere and will disappear as fast,' Matilda said suddenly.

'I have no plans to disappear.'

'But do you have plans to stay?' Matilda said suddenly, allowing the ale to talk.

They continued in silence and Finn let go of Matilda as she opened the door. She was mumbling her thanks and pushing the door shut when she thought she heard Finn say softly, 'I do now.'

Maybe she imagined it. Matilda fell onto her bed, still fully clothed, and began to snore.

Matilda woke with a start, her head thumping. She'd never drunk so much ale in her life and her mouth felt as if it were filled with sand. She desperately needed a drink.

It must have been very late, given the silence. But once she'd drunk her fill of water, Matilda was wide awake. She wouldn't be able to go back to sleep right away. She sat near the window and lifted the shutter to see if it had rained. For once there was a clear sky and she could see the stars above. A full moon cast its light on the ground. Matilda opened the shutter further. There was Thom, dozing happily.

A movement caught her eye. She couldn't make out what it was, an animal or a person. If it was an animal it was certainly a large one. She leaned forward and stared into the dim light. There was definitely something there and it looked as if it was trying to move unnoticed given how it stealthily crept along a short way and hesitated before moving further. Fascinated, she continued to watch as the shape came close. It was almost on the path in front of her house when it stopped and looked directly at her. Matilda gasped and drew back. And carefully and silently she pulled the shutter back again just enough to be able to see out.

Finn was looking at her house and it felt as if they had locked eyes. From his lack of reaction it appeared that he couldn't see her. He wouldn't expect anyone to be looking outside at this time – why should he?

What was he doing?

He turned away and began to walk back towards Agnes's house. Matilda blinked. One moment he was there, and the next he wasn't. Now uncaring whether he saw her or not, she flung the shutter wide open to stick her head outside.

There was no sign of Finn. *How had he moved away so quickly?*

All Matilda could see was a fox with his tail held high, strolling across the green in front of her house as if he owned it.

The ale must still be in my head, Matilda decided. She rubbed her eyes and the fox turned in her direction, glanced at her briefly and continued its walk.

Matilda pushed the shutter firmly closed and tumbled back into bed, dropping immediately into a deep and dreamless sleep.

The beast opened its mouth to howl at the moon but thought better of it. *Why warn its prey?* It glanced from left to right and confirmed it was walking alone. And then it padded slowly to the tree at the side of the path where the branches stopped the moonlight from revealing the glint in its eyes.

Maybe not tonight. But it had patience. The beast scratched its ear and made itself comfortable. It could wait. And if tonight it failed to catch its prey, there was always tomorrow. There was always another day, another opportunity.

It was hungry.

CHAPTER 12

Late winter 1315

In months gone by, Adelaide would have gasped at the sight of dark and sunken eyes in such a white face. She would have demanded that the cotton wrapped around the girl's face was moved aside so she could better see her. But she did not want to see more. She fancied that if she shook the girl, her bones would rattle. Emma shuffled her feet, waiting for her mistress's instructions, looking curiously at the screen near the back of the room.

'His lordship isn't here,' Adelaide said for the second time.

Emma sniffed. 'He won't want to go. He'll want to talk to you.' And she looked longingly at the fire which was now crackling and spitting happily.

'Bring him in,' Adelaide said as she sat demurely on the bench next to the fire. With a little care, she could send him on his way before Robert returned.

Without a word, Emma turned and left the room.

Although the rain had stopped, it had done so only

for long enough for it to be replaced by sleet and then snow. And the snow had fallen and fallen relentlessly until it had started to form drifts and pile up against the walls of buildings. Robert had been fretting about the horses for days now, and had been in the stables for over an hour doing the Lord alone knew what. The stable hand had the flux again – for the third time this month – and was of no use to anyone. But what was to be done? There were no more blankets to be had and not enough wood to think of lighting fires for the animals.

Adelaide hadn't ventured outside for three days now. The last time she'd done so, a magpie had lain dead in her path, its body pulsing with maggots. Emma had shrieked and called out that it was an omen and then she'd wept and said that a child would surely die.

'What do you mean?' snapped Adelaide.

'A creature in league with the devil,' Emma wailed, wringing her hands. 'It carries a drop of his blood on its tongue. It speaks to those who cut its tongue. And it tells of death.'

Adelaide leaned forward and inspected the magpie more closely. She gasped as Emma grabbed her and pulled her away. 'Mistress, you court trouble,' she said.

Although Adelaide had scolded her sharply, her heart wasn't in it and they'd returned indoors. Emma had scurried to the kitchen as soon as she was released and Adelaide had returned to her rooms where she'd thrown a large blanket over her shoulders and curled up as small as she could. This was how she spent most of her days.

Except when Robert was there, of course. But more and more often he wasn't. There was always a small battle to be fought. Someone who'd paid no rent or someone who'd claimed land to which they had no right – and they had so little to sell. The few pigs they kept would have usually been enough to see them through the winter but they now had the scab.

There was a noise at the door and Adelaide stood to greet her visitor. Emma poked her head through, signalled behind herself and disappeared. Adelaide pushed down the fury that threatened to burst out of her. *What was the girl thinking?* She should have remained by her side.

She stifled a gasp as the fattest man she'd even seen in her life fixed his piggy eyes on her. Not only was he fat, he looked as if someone had prepared him for baking; he glistened with oil. And worse, he stank of decay and of want. And he wheezed as if he'd walked twenty miles or more. Maybe he had. He pulled back his cloak and she noted his tonsure.

'You come with news?' she said briskly.

'I come to beg your generosity,' the man wheezed.

'We gave to the King only three weeks ago,' said Adelaide. It was a pointless statement. If the King needed money, the King would take money from them. No one had the strength to argue – hunger had taken that away with so much more. That didn't stop the muttering that the King had little love for his country, that even his own men despised him.

'Not for the King,' the man said, shaking his head determinedly. 'For the church. I come from the monastery.'

Adelaide raised her eyebrows. 'Don't you have stores?'

'Our stores are becoming low – and we have already sold the relics,' the man said hastily as if Adelaide was about to accuse him of hoarding relics as well as food.

'You have more food than us, I warrant.'

'And we have more people making a demand on it,' the man implored modestly. 'Every day we have people banging at our door. They think the church has an obligation to see them fed.'

'And you don't?'

The man shrugged. 'We feed who we can, but it is not our place to fight the will of God. He must make his judgement on the sinful.'

How pious Adelaide thought. 'We starve for our sins?' When the man didn't answer, Adelaide continued, 'But doesn't God command that you care for the people who ask your aid?' She felt herself getting more and more annoyed.

'We do what we can,' he softened.

'And what is that?'

'We have said masses for the sheep and pigs. And we have prayed to Saint Elgius that the farriers will keep health so the horses are cared for. And we walked barefoot in procession to beg God's mercy.'

'Did that fill many bellies?' Adelaide asked scathingly. 'Or did the indulgences you asked for the masses only keep your bellies full?'

'People need to reap the rewards for their sins,' the monk insisted, his face flushed with anger.

'I have nought to give you,' Adelaide said.

'No, m'lady. But once his lordship returns...'

Adelaide sighed. Robert would probably give the monk money to make him go away. And despite her distaste for the monk, he'd be right to offer money. Who knew when they might need the church's help? In these desperate times it would be better to keep as many doors open as possible. After all, this was where the country's real power lay.

She edged past the monk and opened the door. Emma was nowhere to be seen but the young boy Robert had recently taken on waited outside, eager to be given a task. Adelaide crisply told him to take the monk downstairs that he might warm himself in the kitchen and to tell Robert as soon as he returned that he must speak with him.

'The hand of God is raised against us,' said Adelaide as the boy left.

The monk simply nodded.

Adelaide returned to her bench and said, 'You may come out now, Master Edmund.'

An elderly man edged out from behind the screen, stroking his long white beard pensively. 'They don't usually demand money from you in your own home,' he observed.

'No, they don't. I'd warrant he had another intention. Perhaps it was as well that you stepped back. Emma won't say anything.' She gestured and the man pulled up a small stool and sat opposite her.

'God in his mercy has given us full warning,' Edmund said. 'We simply need to know how to read the signs.'

'You were talking of the blazing stars.'

Edmund nodded. 'As I said, the first message was two years ago. Six months in Virgo. Could there be a clearer sign of famine?'

'But this new blazing star?'

'It has been seen clearly. I have received multiple messages. And it arrived with Saint Thomas's day.'

'So that is why people have ignored its message?'

Edmund nodded sadly. 'Indeed. Doubt. All is doubt.' He took a deep breath before continuing. 'M'lady, I would that I had better tidings. But the stars only confirm what we can see around us. They say that people are starving and eating the bark from the trees. And in some places people have fought over the bodies of thieves from the gallows and eaten them.'

Adelaide shuddered. 'So much suffering.'

Edmund pulled out some papers from where they were buried within his tunic and stared at them. 'It appeared while Mars was in Leo and making an opposition to Saturn. It is this that generated the blazing star. And the backwards motion forced this opposition to repeat. Mars brings corrupt blood and unnatural choler, dissension and a scarcity of good faith, and the star's tail points to that planet.'

'But you can make me a charm against the hunger? You can offer something to protect this household?'

'I can give you a charm that will help. But none can

escape this. It's too powerful. Saturn has brought cold and caused seeds to fail. It will continue until he has completed his course and Jupiter gently smiles upon us. The floods of rain will cease, and the land will be filled with plenty, and fields, rich in corn.'

'When?' Adelaide asked eagerly.

'Some three years yet. And worse, there will be drownings.'

For the first time, Adelaide looked at Edmund with scepticism. 'We are not close to the sea. I am less concerned with drownings.'

He shrugged. 'You will be concerned if fishermen can't bring in their haul. Here.' He handed Adelaide a folded piece of paper. 'It has the right words and symbols upon it. Wear it close to your body. You may still be hungry but this will chase away any danger.'

Adelaide tucked the piece of paper down the front of her gown, patting it to make sure it was held securely. 'Praise God that there have been no deaths here,' she said. 'Save of the very old and their time had come, anyway. None of the young have died. They will struggle but we will survive.'

'Some will die,' Edmund said gloomily. 'And I must now depart.'

'You will return after twelfth night?'

'And I will send notice if there is news before.'

Edmund stood and bowed to Adelaide as she got to her feet. 'Do you want me to send your girl to you as I leave?' he asked.

'I would be grateful,' said Adelaide. And she reached in her skirts and retrieved a small purse which she handed to Edmund. Without a word he secreted it within his tunic. He bowed again and Adelaide watched him leave.

Within a few minutes Emma appeared. 'Mistress,' she said dully.

To Adelaide's surprise, Emma appeared to be weeping. 'Speak, girl,' she said impatiently. 'What ails you now?'

'There was a message,' Emma said haltingly between sniffs.

'Indeed, and the messenger has now gone,' Adelaide said impatiently.

'Another message,' insisted Emma. 'A message for me.'

'And what was that message?'

'My mother… she sent a message to say—'

And Emma began to howl. Adelaide grabbed her by the shoulders and shook her hard. 'What message? Why do you weep so?'

'My mother has my son…'

Adelaide's blood ran cold. 'And what has become of him?'

'God has taken him,' Emma wailed. 'He has faded away.' She glared at Adelaide. 'I told you it was an omen.'

'Everything is an omen,' said Adelaide crossly. 'But no one knows what the omens mean until it's over and then it's too late to do anything.' She tossed her book aside and sighed.

Matilda nodded absently.

'What good is an omen that no one can read?' persisted Adelaide.

'I've finished this,' said Matilda, laying down the cloth in her hands. 'Do you want me to begin that veil you were talking about?'

'No – yes – It isn't important, but I suppose you'd better be sewing something if someone comes in. It's in the basket. Maybe some flowers on it?'

Matilda rummaged in the sewing basket, retrieved the veil and threaded her needle.

Adelaide suddenly grinned at Matilda. 'I remember what I was telling you last time you were here,' she said. 'About that day when Nyle walked to the market in the snow and back again just because I wanted a new cap and he had promised me one. It was so cold but he said he didn't feel it because he held me in his heart to keep him warm. He was so – *able*.'

'None of us is able when attacked by footpads.'

'Footpads…'

Matilda looked at Adelaide curiously. 'Did they never find who was responsible? Who did it?'

'You have to look to find,' said Adelaide. 'And look further than the end of your nose. And they aren't the same thing. I don't know who did it but I do know who was responsible.'

They both jumped as the door was flung open and

Robert entered with a peevish look on his face. 'You're late,' he said shortly and exited again without further explanation.

'Responsible,' said Adelaide, staring at the door.

CHAPTER 13

October 1316

Matilda rubbed her bleary eyes and dragged herself from her bed to open the door. Another round of banging began and she snatched it open to see Maerwynn poised with her fist in the air. 'I thought you'd never wake up!' she exclaimed.

'Is it late?' Matilda asked, trying to cover a yawn.

Maerwynn pushed her back indoors, shaking her head. 'I've been waiting for you since the sun came up. Get dressed.' She sat on the chair and watched as Matilda silently did as instructed. 'Are you sick?' she asked.

'No,' said Matilda in a muffled tone as she pulled her tunic over her head. Her face emerged and she offered Maerwynn a weak smile. 'I'm so tired all the time.'

'We all feel tired. And hungry.'

'Yes, but—'

'But nothing. You promised that you would be with me early.'

Matilda yawned. Maerwynn was no doubt telling

the truth, but she couldn't remember having made such a promise. In fact, she'd barely seen Maerwynn over the last few weeks. There'd been other nights at Agnes's home; the company wasn't always the same but Finn was usually present. And the words that came from Agnes's mouth! So tempered with spite and resentment once the ale loosened her tongue. No one else seemed to mind, although once in a while Finn offered Matilda a rueful glance.

'Matilda!'

'I'm ready.' Matilda still wasn't sure what she was ready for.

'Get your basket,' Maerwynn said before walking out of the door without glancing behind to see if Matilda was following. She was, although she stumbled in her efforts to keep up with Maerwynn who was walking at a fast pace, clearly determined to make up for lost time.

As they reached the end of the track out of the village, Matilda saw Finn approaching from the opposite direction. He didn't stop to speak but simply offered a smile. Maerwynn stopped suddenly and turned, watching Finn's back as he walked away. Matilda almost crashed into her and skidded as she stopped.

'Why did he smile at you so?' Maerwynn asked, still watching Finn. He'd nearly disappeared from sight.

Matilda gaped at her. 'So? He was offering a greeting, no more.'

Maerwynn said nothing but turned to continue walking. Matilda grabbed her arm. 'You don't like him.'

'I don't know him – nor do you.'

'I know him enough. And we knew nothing of you when you first arrived and we have become firm friends.' *In truth,* thought Matilda, *I still don't know about Maerwynn's past. Perhaps one day she will trust me enough to tell me.*

Maerwynn hesitated before continuing. 'There is something... strange about that man. I can't put my finger on it but it worries me. Do be careful, Matilda.'

Matilda opened her mouth to argue but thought better of it. For Finn was strange, that was true; she understood what Maerwynn meant. But it was a strangeness that called to her.

'Don't gape like a fish,' snapped Maerwynn.

Matilda raised her eyebrows. 'You're so cross today,' she observed.

Maerwynn looked crestfallen. 'I know, I need something to eat. My belly's growls make me so angry. But he *is* a strange man and people are talking about you and him.'

'They used to talk about you when you first arrived,' Matilda reminded Maerwynn. 'And what do the gossips have to say this time? What fantastic tales have they spun?'

Maerwynn patted Matilda's arm. 'I know the nights are long and lonely, especially when you have been used to having another next to you for so long. But it isn't wise to invite the first man who offers you a smile into your bed.'

'Who said such a thing?' Matilda laughed. 'I am not a child and there's no need for people to think ill of me. Besides, I can bring whomever I like into my bed. Finn has helped me with Thom, and he chopped me some firewood one day. We've shared an ale or two but…'

'It is what people are saying,' Maerwynn answered, dumbfounded by Matilda's fire. She had always thought her a good girl, sometimes a little meek and petulant, but never brazen like this. *I can bring whomever I like into my bed.' Why would she say such a thing?*

'What people?'

'Joan, for one. You've spent quite a bit of time with her lately.'

Matilda shook her head. 'She's wrong. And she knows this. She knows this well.'

'Her mouth always did move faster than her mind,' observed Maerwynn. 'You need to take care. Joan has a knack for saying things that make her look good and others bad.'

'Has she done that to you? Is that why you don't like her?'

'She – It isn't important. It was a long time ago.'

Maerwynn pursed her lips and Matilda decided it was better not to ask more. 'People say strange things in strange times,' Matilda said musingly.

'What do you mean?'

'Nothing but… It was the ale, no doubt it was the ale.'

'The ale made you sleep heavily? Is that so strange?' Maerwynn arched her eyebrows in mock disapproval and Matilda laughed.

'Not that. I saw something… I woke in the early hours a few weeks ago, and looked out of the window.'

Matilda hesitated before committing to tell Maerwynn the tale. She was her good friend after all, it wasn't like she'd trust anyone else with this. They would think her mad if she did. But against her good judgement continued, 'I saw something. I thought it was some kind of beast. It came so close to the house and looked at me that I jumped back.'

'And is that strange? Beasts prowl. It's part of the nature of a beast.'

'That wasn't the strangeness. I looked out again and Finn was outside looking into my house. But he didn't see me and when I blinked he was gone. There was only a fox.'

Maerwynn stared at Matilda. 'The ale made you believe that Finn and a fox were the same?'

Matilda shivered. 'It must have been the ale,' she said weakly. Until Maerwynn had said it so clearly, she hadn't allowed her mind to believe such a thing. *It was nonsense. An impossible thing.* But she knew what she'd seen.

'That's a better story than any Joan has offered for a while,' Maerwynn said. 'A good tale for exchange.'

'I'm being foolish,' Matilda said. 'Ale makes anyone foolish.'

They'd reached the woods and Matilda followed Maerwynn as she walked through a dense patch until they reached a clearing. She gasped. There was a bush rich with berries. Her mouth immediately began to water and she grabbed a handful, shovelling them straight into her mouth. Maerwynn grabbed her hand. 'Slowly. Your belly will thank you.'

Matilda nodded and ate more berries, but at a considered pace. Maerwynn did likewise. Once they'd sated their hunger, without speaking they began to pick the remaining berries and drop them into their baskets. When the bush was empty, Maerwynn signalled that they should move further into the woods. A few moments later, she dropped to the ground and moved a log to reveal a clump of mushrooms.

'These are good to eat,' Maerwynn said. And we can gather nettles and boil a soup. We'll eat well today.'

'How did you know this was here?' Matilda asked.

'I've been watching. But we need to beware of gathering things too soon.' Maerwynn glanced at Matilda. 'It would be as well for you to tend this spot. It's much closer to your home than mine.'

By the time they were ready to leave, they were both carrying full baskets. Maerwynn stopped and picked up some fallen twigs and kindling. 'Lay these atop of your basket,' she said. 'If someone sees we are carrying food, they'll demand their share. We can't be so generous. It's better if they think we're gathering wood.'

They were close to Matilda's house when they saw Finn for the second time. 'It's as if he follows you,' said Maerwynn. 'What *is* his business here?'

'I don't know. He's never told me.'

Finn reached them and offered a low bow. 'It is a fine day,' he observed.

'For a time,' Maerwynn said briskly. 'But we need to get indoors before the rain arrives again.'

'You have done well,' he said, looking into Matilda's basket. She followed his gaze. It was covered in twigs and scraps of wood. Unable to help herself, she smiled broadly at him.

Maerwynn looked questioningly at Finn. 'I can smell what lies beneath the kindling,' he said.

'Come,' said Maerwynn to Matilda. 'We need to attend to our *kindling.*' She began to walk away.

'You'd better follow,' said Finn.

Matilda nodded. Perhaps Maerwynn would explain why she disliked Finn so, when they were both indoors. She turned away but then had second thoughts. Matilda spun round and tapped Finn's arm. 'Would you come and share a soup with me later? I have nettles.'

'It would be a delight,' Finn said gravely.

The delight will be mine, thought Matilda as she turned away again, hiding the grin that was spreading across her face. Although she'd told Maerwynn the truth before, a small part of her wished she had been lying.

That evening, when Matilda was alone again, Finn arrived. 'I've brought you a gift,' he said. 'Close your eyes.'

She complied and he pressed something into her hand. It was wrapped in a small piece of cloth. Eagerly,

Matilda unwrapped it. Nestled in the cloth was a piece of yellow amber, attached to a thin cord. She stared at it in awe.

'It's made from the sun's tears,' said Finn. 'You may wear it around your neck to bring the sun closer to you and bring you joy.'

Immediately, Matilda fastened the cord around her neck. 'I've never been given such a gift,' she said.

'You offered me food. I couldn't come empty handed.'

As if Finn had given her an order, Matilda immediately turned to the pot on the fire and spooned some of the soup she'd prepared from nettles and berries into two bowls. 'It isn't much,' she said.

'In these times, every meal is a banquet.' Finn sat next to Matilda in front of the fire and they supped in silence. The rain was falling more heavily than it had for days and a high wind howled. The shutters rattled and Matilda shivered.

'Were you outside my house that night after you sang?' she asked suddenly. 'After you walked me home?'

'You are alone,' said Finn enigmatically. 'And sometimes I have been concerned for your safety.'

'So that's why you're here? To watch over me?' Matilda spoke in a joking tone despite the curiosity she was fighting.

'I don't know why I'm here,' said Finn. 'Isn't it enough that I am?' He stared into the fire before turning to offer Matilda a smile. 'Tell me a tale.'

Matilda laughed. 'I don't know any tales.'

'Of course you do. Tell me a tale of when you were a child.'

Pictures immediately sprang into Matilda's mind. She could feel the heat of summer days, the smell of newly cut grass, of hay gathered into heaps. She could hear birdsong and her mother's voice.

'I was happy,' she said simply. 'I carried my poppet wherever I went. Mama had made it for me when I was tiny and it had tiny buttons for eyes. I sang to it to lull it to sleep and I wrapped it tightly in my shawl when the winds blew hard. And I would tell it my secrets.' Matilda paused. 'I missed it so much when it was lost.'

'You left it behind somewhere?'

'No! It wasn't lost in that way. I was watching men gather the harvest and had set it aside awhile. When I turned to pick it up again, a goat was looking at me with its devilish eyes and my poppet's legs sticking out of its mouth. I grabbed at it but the goat was fast and not ready to give up its treasure. It gobbled it down as I yelled at it. Mama said she'd make me another but never did. She probably thought I was too old for such games.'

Matilda stared into the distance for a moment and said, 'I wished such evil on that goat. And it ran into a cart the next day and broke three of its legs. We all ate well.'

Finn laughed. 'Tell me more.'

And she talked and talked while Finn watched her. Finally, Matilda held up a hand. 'Enough. I've talked for so long and you've said not a word. I am surprised you haven't fallen asleep.'

'I like to listen to you,' said Finn.

Matilda stared at him. Then she talked some more and Finn watched her with a gentle smile on his face.

It was late when Finn finally left.

As she crawled into bed, Matilda felt bereft. The wind still howled but she stroked the piece of amber and it brought her solace. She'd wished Finn had stayed with her that night, the excitement at that thought thrilled her and she contented herself with dreams of Finn.

Matilda awoke with a start. The moon was still high and its light penetrated the cracks in her doors and shutters, bathing her weather-worn skin.

Howling, snarling; the scream of a fox?

Silently she moved to the window but pulled back her hand from the shutter as another round of louder screaming began. *That of an animal?* she thought. Heart pounding, she opened her shutter, just little enough to peak outside. All seemed still and undisturbed.

Fighting noise broke the silence once more.

Filled with a sense of dread, she resolved to close the shutter and slide back into bed, trying to make as little sound as possible. *If the beasts can't hear me, perhaps they'll leave me alone?* she wondered, as if she were still a child, hiding beneath her bed sheets. It sounded so close she felt her walls would crumble around her bed at any moment.

She stayed still and awake long into the night. The noises ended as suddenly as they had begun, but sleep did not meet her tonight.

CHAPTER 14

March 1316

'We have enough to spare,' Roger insisted.

He lies, Matilda thought. But that wasn't important. Hunger was more powerful than pride. 'I will be in your debt,' she murmured.

'Stay here and I'll be back soon with something to eat. Won't be much, mind,' he said. He took a deep breath and stood up from where he'd been crouched on the floor at Matilda's feet, gesturing to indicate she should stay in her chair.

'The Lord bless you, Roger,' Matilda mumbled. She'd have sold her soul for a good meal. But anything to eat would be a good meal at this point. The pottage she'd made three days ago had got thinner and thinner until she might as well have been drinking rainwater. A meal would lengthen her suffering rather than alleviate it. But if she didn't eat, she couldn't care for Galeran. And if he didn't eat soon, he'd never eat again.

She watched numbly as Roger quietly exited.

Galeran groaned softly and Matilda patted his hand. His eyelids flickered and he went so still that she panicked for a moment. Leaning closer, she felt his weak breath on her face and sighed with relief.

The fire was getting low so she struggled out of her chair, rubbing at her aching back. *How many hours have I been sitting with Galeran?* She opened the door and looked upwards. The sun was just past its highest point. Still a few more hours of daylight.

Galeran wouldn't notice if I walked away, she thought. *If I left everything and walked until I could walk no longer. If I walked until some kind person offered me food, warmth …*

She couldn't imagine losing him or being on her own. She was so frightened for them both.

… But there was nowhere to go.

Matilda went indoors, still rubbing her back. The fire had started to die down so she flung some kindling on it and poked it unenthusiastically. The pile of kindling was woefully low. It wouldn't last more than a day or two and the days remained so cold from the night. *I could burn the stool. Ugly old thing.* She couldn't remember now where they'd got it from – a wedding gift from someone. It was old then. A ragged cushion on its seat made it bearable to sit on, but it would be more use as firewood for an hour its whole life as a stool she thought, growing more and more annoyed with the sight of it. There was still a chair if she needed to sit down and she could sit on the floor. *Better to sit on the floor and be warm than on a stool and freeze.*

The fire burned brightly and Matilda sat next to Galeran, taking his hand in hers. He lay unmoving. Unsure what else to do, Matilda began to sing softly, quietly to him as if he were a baby. After a few minutes she felt foolish and stopped. She wrapped her shawl around herself tightly and yawned.

The sun shone brightly and the meadow was filled with flowers. Matilda laughed happily.

'Come,' said Galeran, taking her hand. 'Come, let's sit by the river.'

They ran hand in hand through the field until they reached the river bank where they both dropped to the ground, trying to catch their breath. Matilda pulled off her shoes and dangled her feet in the river. 'It's so warm,' she said.

'After all these days of sun, what do you expect?' said Galeran. 'Look, I've made you a crown fit for a princess.'

Matilda turned to look and Galeran held out the chain of flowers he'd made and leaned forward to place it around her neck. But he couldn't reach. He was too far away. And he was getting further away. 'Galeran?' Matilda moved towards him but she couldn't reach him. 'Galeran! Stop!'

Galeran's mouth opened into a big O. He held out the chain of flowers beseechingly. His mouth moved but Matilda couldn't hear any sound from him. She began to weep.

Suddenly, she was able to grab the end of the flower

chain. She pulled at it and Galeran moved closer. Filled with relief she pulled as hard as she could until Galeran's face was only inches from her own.

But it was no longer Galeran's face. It had yellow eyes and was covered in hair. And its breath stank. The creature opened its mouth, showing long, yellowing teeth that dripped blood. It growled and lunged at Matilda. She screamed.

Blinking in panic at the strange noises, Matilda realised that she must have fallen asleep. Roger was bustling around the room with a sack held tightly in his left hand.

'What are you doing?' Matilda asked in confusion.

Roger gave a start and laughed. 'I thought you were still sleeping. I was looking for your cooking pot.'

Matilda shook herself fully awake. 'It's next to the fire. I need to throw out the remains – they've been there much too long.' She thought suddenly of eating and her mouth began to water. 'You brought food?' she asked while rubbing her eyes.

Roger looked extremely pleased with himself. 'I have a couple of carrots, beans and' – he proudly held it aloft – 'a turnip!'

Matilda smiled despite herself. 'A turnip? I never thought I would be so pleased to see a turnip. You sit with Galeran and I'll prepare the meal.'

'I won't eat,' said Roger. 'You need to keep what you have for you and Galeran. But I will sit with him.'

117

It didn't take long before the food was ready to eat. Matilda guiltily shoved a few mouthfuls down before taking a bowl and straining some out for Galeran. Carefully, she mashed it into a paste as she would have for a baby. Hopefully, she would never know a baby of her own. *What a terrible thing to think, especially at this time!*

'Shall I feed him?' asked Roger. 'You can take more for yourself. It looks as if you need it.'

Matilda nodded, her heart warmed by Roger's kindness, and passed the bowl to him. She watched as he carefully spooned some between Galeran's lips. Poor Galeran. His lips were so dry that they bled at the lightest touch, although she'd been vigilant in wiping them with a damp cloth. And he dribbled and drooled constantly. There was nothing to be done about the added sour stench this brought. But she was used to the smell, now. She'd been battling to keep Galeran clean since he'd fallen ill – no one wanted to lie in a bed of their own shit and piss. At first he'd managed to drag himself out of bed to do his business. And Matilda had brought the pot to him when he signalled. But for the last two days he'd simply lain still and she'd had to clean him as best she could.

Roger was persistent but little food made its way into Galeran's mouth. Finally, he admitted defeat and came to sit next to Matilda on the floor in front of the fire.

The cold filtered in through every crack in the door, roof and window frame so Matilda moved closer to Roger so they could share what warmth the two of them had. It would be good to be able to talk with someone.

'It's hard for everyone,' Roger said, 'but I've heard that things are worse here than in other places.'

I don't care about other places! Only this place. Matilda tried her best to place a concerned expression on her face.

'So many souls are being taken. God is anxious to meet them sooner.'

'It's a hard time.'

'But not all are being taken by the hunger,' Roger said.

'Like Galeran, you mean? There is much pestilence in the village?'

'No... Do you remember Edward's oldest boy, from Overton?'

Matilda nodded. 'He must almost be a man now. Such a handsome boy.'

'He was found dead. Face down in a ditch. Only two nights ago.' Roger paused. 'What was his name? I can't recall it.'

'Edward. He was also called Edward. What happened to him?'

'He had a huge... clawed... rips down his gullet. Bigger than a wolf's claw.' Roger shuddered. 'He was soaked in blood. Some mad beast had done for him.'

Matilda gasped and her hand shot to her mouth. 'No!' She recalled what she'd heard about Edward before. 'Are you certain it is true because—'

Roger held his hand up to silence Matilda. 'I know what you are going to say. That it was someone he owed money to. It's true he liked the dice. And he lost more money in a wager than he should. But no human could treat another in such a way – save a madman. This had the mark of a beast. Parts of him had been eaten.'

'You saw it? You saw his body?'

'Someone had to bring him in for laying out,' Roger said flatly. 'But I didn't look closely. Just at his face for a brief moment.' Again, he shuddered. 'The poor soul. Terror was burned into his face and his hands were as claws. His nails were broken and he'd obviously tried to fight back – to no avail. They had to cover his face while they laid him out.'

Roger was staring fixedly at the wall, as if Edward's body was suspended there. He coughed briefly. 'But I can't stay. There's work to be done.'

He got to his feet and looked at Matilda in concern. 'I can call later – to see if all is well.'

'No need,' said Matilda briskly as she got to her feet. 'It's likely that Maerwynn will call later, anyway.'

'Do you have a knife near you?'

Confused, Matilda indicated the knife she'd used to chop the vegetables.

'Keep it near you. There may be a madman still at large. Galeran couldn't do much to protect you if something troubled you in the night.'

In response Matilda picked up the large knife and slid it down the top of her skirts. 'There,' she said, 'it is close to me if I should need it.'

Unexpectedly, Roger smiled. 'You will be well, Matilda,' he said. 'This time will pass.'

Although Matilda smiled in agreement and gave a

hearty wave as Roger departed, her heart did not agree with her head.

She sat alone in front of the fire, listening to the occasional moans from Galeran. She was still sitting there hours later when the light began to fail and the dark began to press against her door and windows. And the fog's tendrils sneaked through the spaces in the walls.

Maybe there was more than cold and hunger lurking in the fog.

CHAPTER 15

October 1316

Lord Robert de Ayermin peered into the mist. *I will not be bettered by a vagabond. I will hunt him down. He will regret having crossed my path,* he told himself.

Not that he had actually crossed his path – who would dare? But someone had been wandering the woods. Someone had been stealing. Everyone said so and Adelaide had told him that the manor's stores had gaps they shouldn't.

He had to picture the land in his mind's eye. Everything looked the same in this weather. But he knew it well, the ups and downs, where the trees clustered and a horse couldn't squeeze through. In summer each part had its own shade of green, from an almost sandy colour to a lush deep green, as bright as an emerald. And the trees waved thick and succulent leaves as if to persuade the grass to grow ever higher, ever more thickly. In parts, the ploughing revealed soil of dazzling browns and golds, and scattered in the grass were bellflowers, buttercups, cowslips – he didn't know the names of every flower that scattered on the land but he knew its scent and shape.

At least, that is what it looked like before the rain arrived. Nowadays when you looked down from a hill, it was all a muddy brown. Pools of water festered in hollows and sucked up any plants that tried to grow.

In truth, he enjoyed this, though he never allowed his men to see him take enjoyment. He could have been sitting in front of a warm fire, and easily spare men to perform this task for him. But he needed to be seen to take action. That way his men would be more loyal, more thorough if their betters showed them the way to act.

Robert nearly laughed. He needed to beware he didn't start acting like Howard – the pompous fool. To be fair, Howard did make a good reeve and could be relied on. He knew how to be discreet. When Nyle had been found, Howard said nothing but his eyes said more than words ever could. He also made Robert's flesh crawl, especially in the way he looked at Adelaide when he thought no one was watching. He was useful to have around, and loyal as a dog is to his master that keeps him warm and fed, but Robert knew better than to fully trust him.

The mist had surely thickened since they'd set off. Nothing amiss could be seen. In fact, it was becoming hard to see anything at all. The damp air made his hair stick to his neck and that was making him itch. And his leather suit rubbed against his skin with every movement he made. His legs were chafed and his sores had opened up again and were weeping.

Oddly, his mount was uncomplaining today, although only yesterday it had balked when he tried to coax it out into the fields. It had come to learn that the ground was slippery and hardly a day would go by without it stumbling, if not falling. It was frustrating but Robert had to guide it slowly – at the best a fall would leave him soaked in mud and rotting vegetation.

It would be worthwhile once he'd caught the man and could deliver him his deserved punishment.

Turning his head so he could summon the two men behind him and his tall Irish Wolfhounds, their lord pointed towards the thick tree line to the north-west of his land. 'There. Go forward with speed. I will follow.'

One of the men muttered a complaint but Robert couldn't make out his words. He'd make sure to watch him. The two men coaxed their horses to speed up and passed Robert. He followed them with Adam riding alongside him.

'Stay close,' Robert said to Adam.

Adam nodded. Robert wondered why he'd given such a command. Since being made squire, the boy had remained so close that he was constantly tripping over him. In other times, he'd have chosen someone older, someone more tested by life. In these times, fast decisions needed to be made. It had only been a matter of weeks since he'd finally rid himself of his last squire, Mark – the incompetent fool. And Adam's family had been in the employ of the manor for generations.

Slowly, they made their way down the steep bank.

The horses hissed as they struggled to keep their footing on the frozen ground and the dogs began to howl and whine.

That sound. Did I imagine it?

It sounded like a squeal and came from somewhere in the thicket ahead. Robert pulled his horse to a halt. Adam immediately copied him and threw him a querying look. The dogs' whining growing ever louder.

'Did you hear that?' asked Robert.

'I heard nothing.'

'I am certain…' Robert trailed off. There was no point in wasting time talking. 'Come with me.'

He didn't stop to check that Adam was alongside him. Although the mist was now becoming fog and coating the landscape like a blanket, in the wooded areas the close trees created an illusion of visibility. He aimed straight for them, kicking his horse to command it to move faster. Grunting, the horse broke into a reluctant trot.

Robert heard Adam say, 'Move, damn you. Useless beast,' and turned his head to briefly glance at him. Adam's horse had ground to a halt in protest. Before he was able to say anything, Adam yelled a command at his horse and it whinnied loudly and began to speed up. He would be alongside him again shortly.

Adam's horse neighed loudly. Without turning, Robert shouted as loudly as he could, 'Adam! Kick the beast. Make it move. You're falling behind.' As he did so, his horse broke into a canter. The gap between him and Adam was increasing.

An unearthly scream made him pull his horse to a halt. *What in God's name was that?*

The two men he'd sent ahead were no longer in sight. They may not have been far away but between the trees and the fog, it was hard to make anything much out.

He heard a crunching gurgle and immediately turned and pelted into a canter, dodging the dense trees with expert precision. Branches clawed at his clothes in an attempt to hinder him, but he resisted.

Soon he found the source of the noise.

Adam was slumped across a heavy branch that ran from several feet up a tree to the ground, drenched in blood. His head lolled and ripped muscle was exposed, flesh torn from his body by sharp teeth. His eyes stared glassily at Robert; no life remained in them.

Lord de Ayermin cursed below his breath. Such a waste. And now he needed to find another squire. He put his fingers in his mouth and his whistle pierced the air. Then he heard his men making their way back towards him. They gasped as they saw what had happened.

'My lord, should we carry the body back?' a stocky man with greying hair asked. Robert couldn't recall his name.

'No, there's no hurry. Nothing can be done for him. We'll go back and I'll send some men with a cart.'

They rode back to the manor in silence.

Once Robert had explained what had happened and sent someone to Adam's mother to share the sad news, there was a bustle of activity and three men left pulling a cart in silence, their faces grim.

This was a matter for his reeve to deal with, he decided. It was tempting to ride into town himself and speak to a magistrate but that would appear as if he had no confidence in the men he employed. And that could bring more bother than he needed. Plus, he was tired and covered in mud. It would be better to act promptly.

'Where's Howard?' he asked the stable boy who had arrived to take care of his horse.

'I haven't seen him,' the boy said defensively. 'It's early for him.'

Robert shook his head. 'He'll probably still be in his rooms.'

Robert pulled back the sheet to take another look at Adam's bloodied corpse, noticing with repulsion that he looked different from when he'd left him at the foot of the tree. *Were there parts missing?* He thought. It looked as though in the hour or so Adam had been left there part of the muscles from his arm had been torn out and he'd been disemboweled.

The boy nodded in a way that showed he was more concerned with being agreeable than accurate. Robert ignored him and went indoors. Once in his rooms he called for help and changed his clothes, washing the mud from his body and removing the twigs and leaves attached to his hair. Then he went in search of Howard.

His reeve was well known for doing the absolute minimum he needed to do to keep his role. He was better at giving orders than obeying them. Still, so long as things were done well, it wasn't Robert's place to question precisely how they'd been done. Sometimes, he didn't want to know.

No doubt Adam had befallen foul play. He was a skilled rider and familiar with the woods. Such things didn't happen by accident. *It might not have been Adam who was the intended target.* Robert shivered. It could have been him.

He needed to make sure that Howard understood this so he could convince the magistrate. It would be all too tempting to blame what had happened on the beggar-thief he'd been tracking and conclude he'd simply moved on. Action needed to be taken and quickly. A search of the woods – that would be the best idea. Howard could send someone to the magistrate while some men looked through the woods. Hopefully, the men who'd gone to collect Adam's body would have the sense to look around, but that was doubtful. They tended to obey instructions and no more.

He made his way to Howard's room and banged loudly on the door before flinging it open. Howard was sitting at a table facing the door and yelped with shock. A dish lay in front of him, filled with chicken bones. Grease was dripping down his chin and his open mouth revealed he'd stuffed it full of meat.

Where the hell had he got a chicken from? And eating it alone at this time in the morning?

Howard lurched to his feet, wiping his mouth. 'My

lord... has something happened?' He coughed and wheezed as he stared at Robert.

'I have a task for you,' Robert said crisply.

CHAPTER 16

April 1316

Through the thick fog, a familiar figure approached and Matilda's heart lifted. Thom had become painfully thin, but as he relied on grass for sustenance he was doing better than any person in the village, that was certain.

Matilda's weak voice scratched out from her throat. 'Come, boy. Come to me.'

She placed a hand on his flank when he came beside her. He was such a gentle boy and had never suffered an ill day in his life. With the rains and the failed harvests, there'd been few trips to the manor to sell produce, and there'd been fewer trips to market. But there was always work for a strong and good-natured horse such as Thom, and Matilda had lent him to almost all her neighbours at one time or another.

She looked in the direction of the field. The fog prevented her from seeing more than a blur, but that didn't matter. She knew exactly what it looked like. Soggy, with pools of water stinking of rotting vegetation. The few plants that had bravely fought the elements and managed to break through the frozen soil were weak and faded in colour. She would have to eat them because that was the best the earth had to offer, even though they would taste of little more than dust and failure.

Matilda shivered. Never had she known it so cold, so damp. Even old Ralph who could usually be relied on to tell a tale of how it was worse, longer, shorter, colder – whatever the complaint was – in his day had admitted there'd never been such a winter and that he was hoping God called him sooner rather than later.

People passed through the village, fleeing their homes where there was nothing to eat but bark, where the firewood had rotted in the rain, and where pestilence created a new corpse every day. They scavenged in the woods and along the roads, eating anything that grew. Some of the plants repaid them with madness, making them see monsters or as if wasps were stinging every inch of their flesh.

And they told tales like that of a priest being caught with a baby's leg in his mouth, sobbing that the hunger had forced such a sin on him, that the babe's soul had left already so what was the harm? And of how when the villagers had broken down the door of a house after not having seen a family for several days they'd found a woman, thin as a stick, and her young son fixing their hollow eyes on a spot on the wall as her husband's body lay in the corner with bits hacked from him. They'd eaten the eyes first, the boy told them. One for him and one for his mother. Would that help him see God soon like his mother had said?

It could have been so much worse. It was colder further north, and – if such a thing were possible – she'd been told it was wetter to the west. And they lived under a fair lord, there were far worse than Lord Robert de Ayermin out there, like those who turned up in the dead of night and took all the chickens as one she'd heard of.

But surely God had tested them enough? And surely he'd claimed enough souls for this year? But if he wanted to claim another, perhaps he would claim hers.

Matilda was so tired.

Matilda's toes curled, she struggled to pull her legs up to her chest, buried as she was underneath layer upon layer of clothing. What didn't cover Galeran was piled on top of her. The wooden chair wasn't as comfortable as it could have been but that little discomfort kept her from falling into a deep sleep, made her faster to respond to Galeran if he called out.

She picked up the candle next to her and lifted it above the bed where Galeran lay stiffly. Only his head could be seen, topped with a woollen cap. He frowned as if his dream offended him. Each time he exhaled, a cloud hung over his mouth for a few seconds before being claimed by the damp air. His eyes wept a yellow pus and his nose was red and raw with painful splits on his nostrils. And each of his shallow breaths creaked and whistled.

Shadows danced and spun as she moved the candle. No monsters would hide in these shadows; there was nothing for them to feast on.

The fire was low but cast enough heat to make a small difference. Enough to make it feel as if they weren't outdoors. Matilda would need to find more firewood tomorrow.

Three days it had been since Matilda had last eaten. She had stared longingly at the last spoonfuls of pottage and forced them between Galeran's lips. Two days since she'd drunk more than foul water. She'd shared the last cup of ale with Galeran. No doubt Maerwynn would give her more if she asked – Matilda had had no time to brew her own with caring for Galeran – but she hadn't wanted to leave the house. The wind had howled at her last time she'd opened the door to leave during the day, and at the same moment Galeran had let out a long and low groan. She'd taken that as a command to stay.

Matilda slid from her chair and wriggled across the floor towards the fire. Taking up the poker, she prodded at it apathetically. To her surprise the fire revived and flames began to dance happily. She tossed a few dried leaves onto the fire, taking care that they didn't stop the single log beneath from continuing to burn.

Sleep. She needed to sleep. Tomorrow would be the same.

Matilda wriggled back to the chair and grabbed the clothes she'd been covered with before. She curled up on the floor in front of the fire, creating a nest with the clothes, and curled up into a small ball. And then she blew out the candle.

The dark was thick, almost palpable. Galeran's low, rasping breath was the last thing she heard before falling asleep.

Matilda jerked awake. Every bone in her body ached and her head pounded. She blinked to clear her eyes. It was that strange time before the sun rose and the dark fully departed. She attempted to curl up again to regain her sleep and realised: *Something must have woken me. Something has happened.*

Something is wrong.

The room looked the same but it was different; something was missing. She sniffed and coughed. *What was that smell?*

A rancid stink clawed at the back of her throat. Instinctively, she lifted her hand to her mouth.

Something is wrong.

She sat up and her heavy-lidded eyes scanned the room before settling on Galeran. He lay as immobile as she'd last seen him. But now a mustard liquid dotted with red was pooled next to the bed. And more dripped down the side of the bed. *Drip, drip.*

Poor Galeran. It was an accident. He couldn't help it. And he'd be so humiliated when he woke. But that didn't make it smell any more pleasant. Matilda took in a shallow breath, keeping her hand in front of her mouth. She sighed and her belly churned in protest.

In one minute, only one minute she would get up and see to Galeran. She would clean him and tell him how it didn't matter. How she was happy to care for him. After all, he'd have done the same for her. In one minute she'd shake Galeran awake and he'd try to smile at her and she'd be hopeful again that this would end soon. In one minute.

But the thick silence and eerie stillness that clung to Galeran told a different truth.

In one minute she would stand and touch Galeran. And she would know. Matilda froze. If she didn't move and made no sound, perhaps it wouldn't be real.

'I don't want this,' she said aloud. 'I don't want to be here.'

But there was nowhere else for her to be.

She stretched and stood up, walking slowly to the bed. She rubbed her back and then her eyes, avoiding looking at Galeran's face.

In just one minute.

Taking a deep breath, Matilda bent over Galeran and gently stroked his cheek. He was as cold as ice and somehow his skin had a new texture – wax-like. *I could be wrong.* She tapped Galeran and then grabbed his shoulders and shook him. In her mind she saw his teeth rattle in his head. She stood back and stared at him. He exuded the sort of stillness claimed only by the dead.

He'd gone. Galeran's suffering was over. He would be

well. He'd been a good man in Matilda's mind and that was all that mattered.

In a haze, Matilda carefully pulled on her knitted bonnet and leather shoes, and without a glance behind her, she stepped outside.

She gasped as the cold air dived into her lungs. The fog was beginning to dissipate as the sun peeked above the horizon. Stamping her feet on the hard ground, Matilda turned briefly and gently shut the door to trap what warmth remained inside. Then she stepped into the garden and hesitated, grasping the rosemary bush that climbed the wall, Galeran had planted when they first moved to their home.

'Thom?'

There was a shuffling sound and a whinny. *There he is, leaning against the wall.*

'Thom?' she repeated as she stepped towards him.

He opened his eyes wide and stared at her passively. Matilda stretched out a hand and patted him. Thom nuzzled her and Matilda gave him a half-smile. 'I came out to tell you,' she said. 'He's gone now.'

In her heart Matilda felt Thom's pain.

So she said to Thom, 'I'm not sure I can bear it, either. But we must.'

Thom nuzzled her again.

'He's dead,' said Matilda firmly so there could be no doubt. 'He is dead and we are alone.'

CHAPTER 17

October 1316

That morning Matilda washed her face carefully. She took out her good skirt from the box under her bed and gave it a shake. It was musty but still of a good bright red. And she had a few drops of rosewater left to make it smell sweet.

She clutched her belly as it spasmed. It had been a while since she had eaten. And that had only been nettles. Matilda put on her red skirt and smoothed her hair before shovelling it under her cap. Then she looked at her nails. They were split and broken with dirt embedded under them from when she'd scratched at the soil the day before. Agnes had said there were roots they could eat, they just had to dig far enough. And Matilda and Agnes had dug and dug until they were covered with mud and the rain had grown heavier and heavier. Then Agnes had sobbed until she could sob no more. Matilda had simply got up and walked away. For all she knew, Agnes lay there still.

Nothing mattered but food.

It had also been three days since she'd seen Finn. He'd told Agnes he was going to forage in the woods and would come back with something. He hadn't.

She opened the door. The sky was grey with cloud and there was a breeze, but at least the rain had stopped. Matilda walked over to Thom and he gave her a sad whinny. 'From today you carry me. No more ploughs, no more traps,' said Matilda.

It took a few minutes to persuade Thom that she would ride him, but he agreed in the end. He always did, although he looked as dejected as she felt. No doubt his belly pained him, too. They plodded along the path to the end of the village. Every bone in Matilda's body ached. Her mouth tasted foul and her eyes were constantly filled with grit. She shivered. Cold, she was always cold. Even in the sun she felt cold.

There was Roger. Matilda gave him a listless wave and he raised his hand, watching her in puzzlement. Then he stood in front of Thom so he was forced to stop. 'You're leaving the village?' Roger asked as if nothing would amaze him more.

Matilda laughed. 'Of course not! I'm going to the manor. They have stores and we need to eat. We all need to eat.' She paused. 'I will beg if I need to. Someone must ask.' She'd discovered within herself a fighting spirit she never knew she had.

'They won't help,' said Roger.

'But I must try. Someone must try.'

'Do you want me to come with you?'

'That's kind, but it might be as well if I go alone. And you need to work your land.'

Roger shrugged. 'It would make little difference. I turn the soil but there's nothing in it to grow.' He looked around. 'Where's your sweeting?'

'My... do you mean Finn?'

'If that be his true name.'

'I don't know. I have not seen him for days.'

'No,' said Roger. 'You wouldn't.'

He turned to walk away but Matilda called out to him, 'Roger! What do you mean?'

Roger turned back and moved closer so he could speak in a low voice. 'Do you not think it strange that so many have died since he arrived? And that now there is a madness spreading?' And then he shuffled closer so there was no chance of his being overheard, although no one was there to hear him. 'The night he left, someone broke into old Ralph's barn. There was little in his stores but it was probably enough to satisfy that villain. And now Ralph lies in his bed, fading away.'

'It could have been anyone and you believe this to be Finn. Why?'

'I had a pheasant. And it was stolen while it was hanging.'

Matilda's eyes opened wide. 'You had pheasant? To eat?'

'Not for long. I found it wandering and was readying it. I was going to ask you to share, but I turned away for no more than a moment and it had gone. Maerwynn was arriving and she said no stranger had been near – except your friend.'

Matilda had bent so far forward to hear Roger that she was slipping from Thom's back. She straightened up and looked at him doubtfully. 'Finn told me he had seen a beast and to be careful.' Matilda said more out loud then to Roger. 'We can talk further when I return,' she said. She had no time for idle gossip; she expected it from most but not Roger.

It wasn't Emma's place to welcome people to the manor but she was the only one outside when Matilda approached. She was standing still and staring into the distance. She didn't move as Matilda approached and even when Matilda tapped her arm, she didn't react. She simply kept staring ahead.

'Emma?' tried Matilda.

There was no reaction. Emma was as if froze to the ground. Perhaps the madness had arrived at the manor, too. Matilda stepped around her and entered. And she gasped as she walked straight into Lord Robert who was making his way out.

He gave her a glare. 'Are you here to see my wife?'

Matilda made a brief bow. 'I am here to petition his lordship.'

Robert glared at her again before motioning her to follow him back indoors. 'I have a few minutes. Howard is late.' He spat in the corner of the room and flung himself into the well-stuffed chair in front of the fire.

Matilda kept her eyes fixed firmly on the ground as she stood in front of him and hesitatingly made her plea for assistance. 'I beg his lordship to consider sharing the manor's stores,' she concluded. 'Too many are dying for want of food.'

Robert grimaced. 'I don't know why you should believe we have food aplenty to share. The hunger is everywhere.'

Matilda remained still and silent.

'We need our stores to feed ourselves and my men,' Robert added.

Still Matilda remained silent.

'What advantage is there to me if I reduce our meagre stores for the sake of villagers who haven't had the sense to plan? What do I gain from this?'

'Plan? For two years' of hunger and cold? For unceasing rain?' Matilda hissed. Then realising her error in accepting the bait, she lowered her eyes and added insincerely, 'It would be a good thing in the eyes of God.'

Robert laughed. 'And in this life?' He got to his feet and moved so close to Matilda that she could feel his breath on her face. Then he said quietly, 'Though if you were to offer me a payment in kindness, I could consider.'

Matilda closed her eyes briefly and then looked directly into his piercing blue eyes. 'I do not know what you mean.' His hand stroked her arm so briefly that she wondered if she'd imagined it.

'Adelaide does not wish to lie with me any longer.'

'That is sad for you,' said Matilda. 'The hunger has made people act – differently.'

She continued to stare at Robert and then suddenly he backed away and returned to his chair. 'Go,' he said briskly. 'I'll speak with Howard and ask him to assess our stores to see what we may spare.'

Matilda bowed and turned to leave. This was the most she could hope for at this time. And there was still tomorrow. She vowed to return each day until Lord Robert agreed to help. She would have to pay for making such a bold request and his advances frightened her.

Maerwynn was on Matilda's doorstep when she returned. 'I seek sanctuary,' she said gravely. 'Everywhere I go there are tongues wagging about Finn and I've heard more thoughts about him than I can stomach.'

Matilda eyed Maerwynn suspiciously. She was well aware that Maerwynn held no love or kind word for Finn. Matilda knew she was trying to gain favour, but played along anyway, intrigued as to where this was going. 'Come and sit with me awhile.' She patted Thom and led him to the corner of the garden where he stood dejectedly. Then she led Maerwynn indoors to sit by the empty fire.

It seemed that every tongue in the village had wagged in Maerwynn's direction and Matilda's head began to spin as she related the stories she'd heard of Finn's potential sins. 'He couldn't have soured Agnes's milk and stolen Ralph's bread at the same moment,' she pointed out. 'They live at opposite ends of the village!'

'I don't know the truth of it. Only that every time something is laid down and a body turns away, it disappears. And he remains looking healthy.'

'He doesn't look anything now,' Matilda said with exasperation. 'I haven't seen him for days.' Then she thought for a moment. 'But those tales of a beast – I'd give those more merit. I have seen in the shadows…' Her amusement at the gossip about Finn was slowly turning to worry about where this was going to lead. It wouldn't be anywhere good.

'Beast… witches… monsters,' said Maerwynn dismissively. ''Tis the weather that is most to blame. Anyway, where have you been today?'

Matilda explained about her petition.

'You may have had more success if you'd asked her ladyship,' Maerwynn pointed out. 'Though she is a strange one.'

'I do see why Lord Robert wanted her. She is very beautiful.'

'Not the sort of beauty that lies within, I'll warrant,' Maerwynn said darkly. 'All those books have likely addled her brain and put darkness in her heart. And she still isn't with child.'

'I've rarely spoken to her.' Matilda stared at the fireplace as if willing flames to spring forth. 'But what I do know I like. I do not believe she has darkness in her, only light.'

Maerwynn patted her shoulder. 'Talk is all some people have at the moment. Don't fret.'

'Then maybe we should attempt to talk of something different. Tell me a tale. You know many and I miss Galeran's tales.'

Maerwynn nodded and she began.

There once was a man who was compelled to spend three days of each week as a wolf. He kept it secret from his wife for a full year, but she wept each time he departed and cried out that she knew he had another love. He didn't want to tell her lest he lose her love. But then he realised he'd lose it if she thought his heart was given to another. So he told her the truth.

She was much afeared at the start, but he was still her husband so she said she'd honour their marriage vows and remain with him. Nonetheless, the strangeness worried her deeply and she wept many tears when left alone on the nights he prowled the woods.

One morning her husband returned to find fresh tears on her face. 'And what more ails you?' he asked. She confessed that she was with child and fretted that one day he would leave as a wolf and be unable to return to the shape of a man. Her husband told her that she was worrying needlessly. He explained that whenever he'd served his time as a wolf, he only needed to find his clothes to enable him to become human again. Because she asked again and again, he told her of the hollow rock in which he hid his clothes.

And then the man ceased to worry because he could live his life as a man-wolf with his wife's knowledge.

But his wife didn't want to lie with a wolf, and she pleaded tiredness whenever he came to her bed. Truth was, she felt she was in a half-marriage – she didn't have a husband she could depend on but neither did she have the freedom to control her own life.

It came into her mind that it would be better if she were free of her husband. So when a pedlar came by asking if there were any tasks he could do for a few pennies, she gave him a coin and sent him to the woods, telling him to return with the pile of clothes he'd find there.

This the pedlar did. And now the man was cursed to remain as a wolf.

Adelaide yawned.

'Do you wish me to continue?' asked Finn.

'I do,' she said. 'I will pay you well if your tale pleases me.'

So Finn continued:

The woman soon grew used to being alone and gave birth to her daughter. Sometimes she saw a shape among the trees and fancied it was calling to her, but then she dismissed the thought before getting on with her daily tasks. Though each night she locked her door firmly to keep out any beast.

One day she'd been working so hard that she forgot to lock the door. Late that night she was awakened by a banging noise and woke to find a wolf in her house. She was much afraid and grabbed her baby, pleading with the wolf not to harm her.

He growled at her and she realised who he was and ran to the chest in the corner of the room. From there she pulled out her husband's clothes which she had kept. And then the wolf became a man again.

'Why didn't you bring me my clothes before?' her husband cried as he was dressing.

'Your clothes were always here,' she said. 'you could have collected them whenever you wished. And why didn't you return to see your daughter?'

The man sat on a stool and told his wife to bring him an ale and said he was hungry. The woman stared at him for a moment and then she began to laugh. 'Whether man or beast, you are of no use to me if you don't listen to what I say,' she said.

The man grew angry and shouted for more ale. The woman quietly said that when he'd finished his ale he could be on his way as she had a daughter to care for and work to do. The man shouted again but to no avail. And after some time he understood that the shouting made no difference. Then dejectedly he bid his wife farewell for one last time and he left. The woman never saw him again and she lived a happy life.

Finn had clearly finished and Adelaide tossed him a coin. It had been such a good story and she wished she were that wife. Finn immediately tossed the coin back to her and she looked at him in confusion. 'You have things of more value to me than coin,' he said. 'You have bread.'

'But we have eaten.'

'And many have not. Pay me in bread.'

CHAPTER 18

October 1316

Finn had a huge grin on his face. Matilda looked past him to see a huddle of villagers standing on the green, staring and pointing.

'Good morning,' she said for want of anything better to say. She felt a surge of joy to see him again that she couldn't hide.

'Indeed, it is a fine morning.' Finn said. 'May I come inside?'

Matilda nodded as she stepped back to allow him to pass. 'For a few moments,' she said. As she turned back to close the door, she could feel the eyes of the villagers on her. She shivered.

Finn was carefully unwrapping a bundle he had laid on the table. Curiously, Matilda moved closer. Then she gasped as she saw the loaf within the bundle and immediately began to salivate. 'Bread!' she said. 'You have brought bread.'

She moved a hand towards it to grab a piece and then hesitated.

'I brought it to share,' Finn said gently. 'Take some.'

Eagerly Matilda broke off a small piece and stuffed it in her mouth. And then another. And another. Then Finn grabbed her hand. 'Not so fast,' he said. 'It will pain your belly.' Then he took a small piece himself and chewed it slowly.

Matilda waited until Finn nodded and took another piece of bread. This time she chewed it slowly as Finn did. He reached further inside his bundle and produced a flask. 'This is a good ale,' he said. 'It will make you brighter.' He took a swig and passed the flask to Matilda and she drank deeply. Then Finn broke the remaining bread into two, handing half to Matilda. They finished it in silence.

'That is the best thing I have ever eaten in my life,' Matilda said before she wiped the crumbs from her mouth and licked her fingers. 'But how did you come by bread? And enough to spare?'

Finn shrugged.

'And where have you been these last few days?'

His grin returned. 'Have you been pining for me?'

Before Matilda could respond, there was a loud knock at the door and someone called her name. She pushed past Finn and opened it to find Roger with his hand raised, ready to knock again.

'You need to come,' he said.

'Has something happened?'

Finn approached and stood behind Matilda and Roger's eyes widened. 'I see you're back,' he said. Then he grabbed Matilda's hand. 'Come, we need to go to the church. There is food. From the manor. You need to get your share.'

Wordlessly, Matilda pulled her arm free and gave Roger a scathing look but she decided not to say more but to simply follow him. Roger led her through her garden and along the path towards the church. Finn followed close behind them. Suddenly, Roger stopped and turned to Finn. 'It may be unwise for you to come with us.'

Finn opened his mouth as if to say something and thought better of it. He shrugged. 'As you wish.'

He turned to walk away and Matilda called after him, 'Call on me later. I would like your company.'

Finn raised a hand to show he'd heard her and continued walking.

Roger tugged at Matilda's arm as she watched him go. 'We need to go.'

Matilda walked alongside Roger in silence for a few minutes. 'Why did you do that?' she asked.

'Galeran is barely cold and that man is at your side every time I look. People are talking.'

'People will always talk. I don't much care to hear what they have to say – and I didn't think you would either, Roger.'

'The moment your husband is dead you invite another man into your bed,' Roger continued as if Matilda hadn't spoken.

'Roger! Do you believe that? Should I spend my time alone?'

'Of course not, but—'

'There is not a but. I am grown. I live or die by my own hand. But I can't speak with who I want?' Fury showed on Matilda's face. She would expect this from most villagers and wouldn't usually care, but from Roger, this hurt her very much.

'None of us can do as we want,' Roger said bleakly. 'The world isn't like that.' Then he sighed. 'I know you must be lonely, but we know nothing about him. Finn isn't one of us. We don't know where he comes from or what he does. And there have been so many thefts…'

'Finn's a thief because he's a stranger?'

'We know nothing about him,' Roger said obstinately.

'But you know much about me,' Matilda pointed out. Then she sighed and said gently, 'I am thankful that you worry about me, but I'm neither your wife or daughter.'

Roger pursed his lips and looked into the distance.

Matilda patted Roger on his arm. 'I am thankful,' she repeated, 'but there truly is nothing you need fret about.'

Roger didn't respond and they completed their walk in silence.

Agnes was standing at the church door, deep in conversation with Peter when they arrived. Matilda waved a greeting but Agnes turned away. Confused, she smiled at

Peter. He acted as if she weren't there and turned to follow Agnes.

'I tried to warn you,' Roger said in a low voice.

They entered the church to be greeted by Howard. 'You must take your turn,' he said and then pointed to the back of the church.

The church was filled by villagers. Some were holding small bundles and pushing their way towards the door. Others were inspecting something at the far end of the church. All were talking loudly. As Matilda pushed through the crowd she heard a few hisses and tuts but when she turned to see who was making the noises she was met only with blank faces or weak smiles.

Howard came up behind her and pushed Matilda aside. 'Don't block my way,' he said crossly. 'You can take one bundle. One only. Then you must step back so someone else can take their share.'

'I don't understand,' said Matilda.

Howard glared at Matilda. 'There is little to understand. His lordship has made an inspection of the manor's stores and decided that there is enough surplus to bestow a gift onto us. I have divided it into bundles so all have their fair share.'

He glanced around to see if anyone was listening and on seeing that no one was paying them any attention, being too busy gossiping, he said to Roger, 'I'd hoped you would be here earlier. I had to make it into bundles. They were grabbing and fighting over what they could get before I did that.'

'People are hungry,' Roger said. 'That's all that fills their minds.'

Matilda saw a gap in the crowd and leaned forward to grab one of the bundles.

'Don't open it now,' said Roger. 'It won't contain any more if you do. Let's go back.'

Matilda turned to do so and immediately tripped over a woman sitting on the floor, oblivious to everything except the carrot she was shoving into her mouth. She got back to her feet and made her way towards the door.

'His lordship is here!' Howard yelled.

Silence fell as Robert walked into the church and surveyed the villagers. 'No priest?' he said.

'I couldn't find him,' Howard said.

Robert looked directly into Matilda's eyes for a moment and she shivered. Then he turned back to Howard. 'Tell them that this is all we have to offer. Then clear the church.' Immediately, he turned to leave.

Howard opened his mouth to speak but before he could utter a word, Peter yelled at him, 'We have ears.'

Roger stepped forward and patted his arm before whispering into Peter's ear. Nodding, Peter began to pull people from the floor where they were sitting and direct them towards the door. Roger inspected the bundles and grabbed one from a young child who was holding two and gave it to Kate who was simultaneously trying to push forward and keep hold of her children.

Within a few minutes the disorderly huddle at the

back of the church had been turned into a line and people were beginning to leave. Lord Robert had left.

Matilda looked around. 'Roger?' she called.

He looked up.

'Has someone told Maerwynn?'

'I believe so. Howard sent people to knock on every door. I was heading for your house anyway so...' He looked around. 'She may already have left.'

'I'll call on her.' Clutching her bundle tightly, Matilda stepped outside. Robert was standing outside, deep in conversation with one of his men. As she walked past him, Matilda bobbed. 'Thank you for hearing my petition,' she said.

To her surprise, Robert laughed. 'This has nothing to do with me. You refused my offer. Although if you wish to reconsider...'

Matilda felt her face grow hot and she bit her tongue hard before any words could escape.

Adelaide was sitting on her horse at the edge of the woods, looking at the church as Finn approached her.

'You did a good thing,' he said.

'I did the only thing,' Adelaide said in response, 'but it isn't enough. Our stores are almost empty. And there's little to buy in town, no matter how much money we offer. I sent two men to the market today but they will likely return with nothing more than a look of satisfaction on their faces.' Then she grimaced. 'And Robert is furious.'

'He'll be happier when he receives the thanks he thinks he deserves,' said Finn.

Adelaide nodded. Then she pointed at Matilda who was walking away from the church, alone. 'That is her?'

'Her?'

'There is someone who makes you remain here and your eyes are drawn to her,' Adelaide said. 'And everyone talks. Emma told me that you are with her as night falls.'

'Not *every* night,' said Finn. 'And not *all* night.'

'But there is always more talk about what people do under cover of darkness,' Adelaide observed. Then she leaned down and lowered her voice. 'You must take care. You're a stranger here. These people aren't happy with strangers, especially any that are different to them.'

'Like you?' Finn asked.

'I'm still a stranger here, and worse, I'm a stranger who can read. The priest told Robert to beware of me. Fortunately, Robert values what the priest says even less than what I say.'

'I'm surprised he allowed you to do this.'

'He didn't,' said Adelaide. 'I sent Emma to tell Howard it was his master's instructions and he was too lazy to check. And Robert didn't want anyone to know he was bettered by his wife. Howard will pay for that mistake – and I'm sure I will too, in due course.'

She stared in Matilda's direction. 'My destiny is decided,' Adelaide said pensively. 'Not yours. Not hers.'

'You can change your destiny,' said Finn.

Adelaide laughed. 'I shall if the opportunity presents itself, but for now I must be satisfied helping others change theirs.' Then she gave her horse's reins a brief tug and he whinnied in surprise. 'I must return. Master Edmund is waiting to see me. Take care, Finn.'

Finn raised his hand as Adelaide rode away. Then whistling, he walked into the depths of the woods.

Robert watched as Matilda walked away. Then he decisively turned his horse and followed her. She didn't turn to look at him as he slowly rode a few yards behind her. His horse shied briefly as it encountered a bush like so many other bushes but bothersome in a way only a horse understood. Robert made a reassuring noise and the horse resumed its slow walk as if nothing had happened. Matilda's thoughts seemed to have consumed her as she didn't turn, but she now walked faster, more determinedly. Robert hardly dared breathe for fear of breaking the spell, although what that spell was he couldn't have said.

When Matilda reached her house and went indoors, Robert dismounted and walked to her door and knocked on it loudly. When nothing happened, he gave it a light push and the door began to open. He saw Matilda's face through the gap and her arm raised as she reached to push it shut again. He pushed it harder and Matilda stepped back as he stepped inside. She reached behind her and grabbed something from the table.

'It's better that we have such conversations in a quieter space,' Robert said, standing only inches away from the door.

Matilda bobbed and then eyed him with suspicion. 'Your lordship?'

'You owe me a debt.'

Matilda felt the blood leave her face. Her boldness was fading now they were truly alone. 'I have nothing of value to pay you with,' she said.

'I believe you do.' He stared at Matilda and she returned his stare. Then Robert reached forward and grabbed Matilda, pulling her close to him. She struggled but was unable to free herself.

'Come,' he said. 'You offer your favours to that stranger. It would do you better to share them where you can gain more reward.' He began to release his hold and gasped as something stung his cheek and then something wet trickled down his face. Matilda took a single step away from him, her knife still in her hand.

Robert laughed and wiped his face. He winced briefly but didn't take his eyes from Matilda for a second. Then he lunged forward and pushed her hard. Matilda stumbled and dropped to the floor. Immediately, Robert dropped to his knees and was leaning over Matilda before she realised what was happening. She stared up at him and Robert shivered as he met her eyes. She struck his face again with the back of her closed fist. He faltered for a moment, then smiled as if incensed by her defiance. Robert grabbed Matilda and thrust his hand up her skirts. She yelped and he thrust his hand deeper until it encountered something wet and slippery.

Matilda hissed at him and Robert instinctively flung himself backward. He glanced at his hand and saw his fingers were covered in blood. Scrambling to his feet, Robert retched and wiped his hand down his tunic again and again. He would burn it as soon as he was home.

She was laughing at him. Quietly, but she was laughing at him. He could see her shoulders shake. More from relief than anything else.

'I will return,' Robert said deliberately. 'I will be here when you are more desirable, less afflicted. And I'll bring my men with me. You can expect some return for insulting me with your knife.'

Robert walked out and Matilda sank lower onto the ground, wrapping her arms tightly around herself.

The full moon cast enough light onto the ground for Peter to easily make his way to the barn without worrying too much about where he put his feet. He hiccoughed loudly and clapped his hand in front of his mouth. That last ale had gone down far too quickly. He glanced around. No one was to be seen. Good.

It was a miracle he'd managed to keep that chicken for so long. Until now, her eggs had been too valuable to warrant killing her, but she'd stopped laying this past week and it was now time. His wife had warned him to take care, not to let anyone see or they'd steal the chicken as fast as he could blink. The hollow eyes of his four children were enough to ensure he listened to her. But they would eat well tonight. No one would call at this hour. No one would know.

A shape moved past at the edge of his vision. He spun around. *What was that?* It had looked like some sort of large beast but he hadn't seen enough of it to be certain. He stared into the darkness but nothing more moved.

Carefully, he opened the barn door. It always squeaked a little but the noise wasn't too much if he moved slowly. Once inside, he blinked. *Where was it?*

Usually, the chicken ran towards him when he entered the barn but there was no sign of it. He made a clucking noise and listened. Nothing. He sighed and opened the door wide to allow the moonlight to enter the barn. Then something gleamed on the floor. He dropped to his knees and inspected it.

Blood.

And next to the blood were a few scattered feathers. Peter dropped his head into his hands and howled.

'You look well,' said Matilda.

Maerwynn smiled. 'And you. Is it that man who has put the light back into your eyes?'

Matilda laughed. 'I wouldn't have expected you to listen to village gossip,' she observed sarcastically.

'I don't need to. I have my own eyes.' Then a dark look

came over Maerwynn's face. 'You need to take care. We know nothing about him.'

'I know enough.'

They sat in silence for a few moments and then Matilda yawned deeply. 'I'm sorry, Maerwynn. It has been too long a day. Will you sleep here tonight?'

Maerwynn nodded. 'If you'd like me to.'

He'd meant to wait until the morning, but fury had been building up inside him since he'd told his wife what had happened. And if he didn't act quickly, the thief would get away and escape justice. Peter had always insisted on justice. His wife and children could attest to what he meant by 'justice' as they often bore the bruises he'd bestowed on them for transgressions.

Within a half hour he was at the manor and Howard was looking at him in puzzlement.

'I don't know what you expect me to do,' he said. 'It's too late now.'

To his astonishment, Peter slapped him. 'You were born a weakling,' he said. 'Your father would be ashamed of you. You need to gather some men and search the village. Someone is having a good meal tonight and if you move quickly enough, you'll find who it was.'

Howard stepped backwards, rubbing his cheek. 'I'll give you two men. And I'll come with you.' Then he grinned. 'It could be good sport.'

It wasn't. After knocking on every door in the

village, the men relented and demanded their beds. Peter returned home, defeated. That night he showed his wife just how defeated he felt.

CHAPTER 19

October 1316

The little girl held the boy's hand tightly. She had a resolute expression on her face, although she was chewing her lip with anxiety. Lord Robert slowed his horse to take a closer look.

The girl paused to glance at him, pulled her brother's hand and continued to walk at a dragging pace. He'd begun to wail but she simply yanked his hand harder when his wails grew louder. Robert drew up alongside them. 'Stop,' he said.

They stopped and looked up at him, waiting. They were younger than he'd first thought; the girl couldn't have been older than five summers and the boy looked barely old enough to walk. Both stared at him, wide-eyed and passive. Robert glanced in both directions. There was no one else on the road and they were at least two miles from the village.

'Where are you going?' asked Robert. He had to yell so they could hear him above the sound of the rain.

The girl pointed along the road towards the town.

'And where are you from?'

She pointed in the direction of the village. The boy promptly sat on the ground and howled as mud splashed up into his face. The girl bent and wiped his face and then looked up at Robert again. When he didn't immediately say anything, she pulled hard on the boy's hand until he was standing and they resumed their slow trudge along the road.

'Stop!' Robert said again. They ignored him. He pulled his horse round to block their path. 'Tell me, why are you on the road alone?' he asked.

'Hungry,' said the girl. 'Mama told us to walk to find food.'

'Where is your mama?'

The girl shrugged and the boy said defensively, 'She *told* us.'

'She told us not to come back,' the girl added. 'She said someone would take us and feed us.' A thought occurred to her. 'Will you take us?'

'I'll take you back to your mama,' said Robert.

Both children began to wail loudly. 'She will beat us!' the boy screamed. 'She said we mustn't come home!'

Robert shivered. 'Then I'll take you elsewhere,' he said pragmatically. 'You can't remain on the road.' He thought for a moment. 'I'll take you to the convent.'

The girl laughed bitterly. 'They closed their doors to us when we went with Mama and begged for a few crumbs. They said there were no crumbs to be had.'

163

Robert believed her. But the children were walking to their deaths. And the convent would open its doors to him – they would welcome him as their lord and would take the children with a smile, even if that smile was forced. He smiled inwardly in satisfaction; this was the action of a good lord.

'Come with me,' he said. And he dismounted and grabbed the boy, setting him on the back of his horse. The boy sighed and waited for Robert to pick up his sister and place her behind him. She gripped onto him tightly. Robert got back onto his horse with the children pressed against his back. He turned to go back to the village and both children began to sob.

They were probably right and he needed to get into the town in any event. He turned around and began to move smartly towards the town. He'd leave the children with the magistrate.

'We saw a wolf,' the girl said suddenly. 'It told us to stay on the road and it let us ride on his back.'

Robert ignored her.

When a horse had died on the road last week, word had spread in moments and nearly the whole village had run towards the road, armed with knives. They'd hacked at the corpse, grabbing what they could, deaf to the protests of its rider who finally gave up and sat at the side of the road, his head in his hands in despair.

Matilda had thought she was hungry before. She'd

thought she knew what hunger was. But this was different. She would no longer lend Thom for fear he'd end up in someone's pot. To her shame she'd looked at him from time to time, calculating how many meals he'd make. All too few now he was so thin and his bones poked painfully from his skin.

None of this stopped her mouth from watering at the thought of horse flesh.

They no longer buried people – just dropped them into pits with perhaps a few perfunctory words. No one had the strength to do more. And it was rumoured that some of the bodies had pieces missing from them by the time they reached the graveyard. No one wanted to check.

Matilda heard a strange sound and stepped outside to see what it was. Joan was standing fully naked, screaming at the sky. Her once shining hair hung in rat's tails at the sides of her face and flies buzzed around her head. Her skin was the colour of spoiled milk and as she screamed, spittle foamed around her mouth. Matilda looked at her in horror. She grabbed her shawl and rushed to Joan to cover her only to be delivered a punch in the eye for her pains. Joan continued to scream, unearthly screams, as if her nightmares had become real. Matilda shuddered and reached for Joan again but after a few slaps she had to give up. Joan continued to rant although Matilda couldn't make out any words.

She stepped away and slowly made her way back to her house. Joan would stop when she grew tired. Matilda didn't have the strength to fight her. She sat in front of her low fire but could still hear Joan's screams until she put her hands over her ears.

And she began to sob.

The previous night, Finn had told her a tale and she relived it in her head. Anything to take her mind off of the screaming:

'There was once a priest who had come across a talking wolf while travelling,' he said. 'The wolf had told him that he and his companion had been compelled by a saint to live in exile as wolves for seven years. When their time was done, two others would take their place.

'"She has reached her time," the wolf said sadly, looking at his companion who lay on the ground, unmoving. "Pray for her."

'The priest dropped to his knees and offered the sacrament to the dying wolf. As he finished and regained his feet, the wolf pulled at its skin to reveal an old woman beneath. The priest gasped with wonder and the woman whimpered and left this world.'

Matilda nodded. 'You can't always see the true person on the surface.' She yawned because she craved sleep but her complaining belly refused to allow it.

Joan was still screaming. And now Matilda could also hear Agnes's raised voice. She ventured outdoors again. Joan was now standing still with her arms by her sides and Agnes wrapped around her from behind.

'Help me get her indoors,' yelled Agnes.

Matilda stepped towards them and helped drag the ranting Joan into her house. Once they were inside, Joan whimpered and curled into a small ball. Agnes threw a cover on her where she lay.

An empty pot was suspended above the cold grate. Next to it, three empty jars lay on the ground.

'That's why she rants so,' said Agnes. 'Someone crept in while she was foraging for nettles and took the little that remained in her stores.'

'But who?' asked Matilda. 'Who would do such a thing?'

Agnes dropped to the floor and took Joan in her arms and began to hum an old nursery rhyme to her as if she were a baby. 'Not one of us. It couldn't be one of us. And there is only one stranger recently arrived.'

'Finn?'

Agnes shrugged. 'There is a beast at large; there is a sinner amongst us. Maybe they are one and the same. But we should not talk of such things. It will only bring more problems.' She began to sing softly to Joan who was now quiet.

Meanwhile, Maerwynn banged again on Matilda's door. *Surely she couldn't still be sleeping?*

'It appears that she isn't there,' a voice observed from behind her.

She span around to see Finn leaning on a low wall and watching her with amusement in his eyes. His cheeks were still full, not sunken like those of the others in the village. And his clothes still bound to his body, not hung like curtains over his bones. In short, he looked as if he didn't lack too many meals.

'I know what you are,' hissed Maerwynn.

'And I you,' said Finn.

Eventually, Joan dropped into a slumber and Agnes and Matilda crept quietly out of her house.

'I can't stay with her,' Agnes said, 'But I'll return later.'

Matilda felt guilty at not offering to sit with Joan but her brain was filled with a fog and her head was beginning to spin. She was afraid the madness was like a pestilence and would take her soon.

As she made her way back home she saw Maerwynn leaving her path and Finn leaning against the wall staring after her.

'Maerwynn,' Matilda called. She wanted to ask her to help Joan.

Maerwynn heard Matilda but was so incensed by Finn's presence she thought it best to just walk away. She didn't want to be drawn into an argument in public with someone like Finn; not after what he'd just revealed to her.

'Why didn't she stop?' Matilda asked Finn.

'You should be careful, things are not always as they seem. That goes for people too.' Finn's eyes didn't leave Matilda, as if he were telling her a very important secret.

'Nothing is as it seems right now. Joan is raving in her bed. And all I can do is think of sleep.'

'Good, you should just stay in tonight,' Finn insisted.

'There is something not right at the moment and I think everyone would fair better in their beds when it becomes dark, rather than running round looking for thieves and solutions.'

Matilda looked at him curiously, not quite understanding what he meant but trusting it was good advice.

The beast howled at the moon and then howled again. The ground was soaked in moonlight and had anyone decided to look, they would have clearly seen the beast as it paced up and down the thoroughfare in the village.

The beast snuffled at the ground. It needed only to wait its moment. Soon there would be blood.

Upon returning Matilda screamed at the sight of Joan's body. She screamed until people came running in and demanded to know what ailed her. To find another body in the morning wasn't so great a shock. To find one naked in the street, coated in blood with pieces torn from it was another matter.

There was a beast amongst them.

CHAPTER 20

October 1316

There was little work he could do that day. Despite the early hour, Roger had already broken his fast with a few mouthfuls of the weak stew that remained in the pot over the fire. He had tidied, although there were few things to move now he'd sold almost everything he owned of value to buy food. Although it was rare that anyone knocked on his door, that anyone but himself would see the inside of his house, Roger still maintained enough pride to keep it clean in case that rare event occurred today.

He'd spent a few minutes attending his garden. A few minutes was more than he needed. Only a sparse number of small shoots resolutely poked through the ground and it had been tempting to pull them from the ground and eat them at that moment. He wasn't even sure what plant was growing. It didn't matter. Anything that grew was allowed its space now. The time for clearing usurping plants was in the past. As long as it wasn't poisonous, it could be eaten. Carefully, he'd cleared mud back from where it threatened to swallow the shoots and pulled away dried leaves that had blown in on the evening wind. Then he'd stretched and rubbed at his aching back. It was pointless – his bones ached, every minute of every day.

The two small sheep that remained of his flock were penned in his garden and looked at him sorrowfully. They wanted to be back on the hills, wandering at whim, but he couldn't leave them unattended. He wouldn't even risk leaving them outdoors unless he was there. He would have to slaughter one in the next day or two.

Going back indoors, Roger sat on his stool in front of the fire and picked up his knife. He rubbed his head and blinked a few times. For a moment, the room swam and he put out a hand as if to still it. Then all was still again. He shook himself briefly and turned his attention back to his task. That branch he'd picked out of the firewood had called out to him to be carved. He'd seen the face within it immediately, and with only a few touches of his knife he'd revealed the body of the woman it had now become. Only a few small adjustments and it would be complete. It was as well not to work too long on a carving. One wrong cut and the whole thing could be ruined.

There! It was complete. And it bore a resemblance to Matilda. He decided to take it to her immediately. He stood too quickly and the room began to swim again. This time, shapes soared around him in a mist and he had to rub his eyes to force them to retreat.

Now having a purpose, Roger didn't want to waste any more time. He coaxed the sheep indoors and set off to Matilda's house. He hadn't seen her for a few days – he hadn't seen anyone for a few days. It wasn't so much that the hunger made him morose, more that the misery on the faces of others hurt his heart and made him want to weep. Sometimes, it was better not to see the faces. But this would bring a smile to Matilda's lips; her smiles warmed Roger's heart. He worried about her; she spent too much time alone. When she wasn't alone, Roger wasn't sure she chose the best companions. Agnes was more interested in drinking than anything – and she had a nasty, sharp tongue when she imagined an offence against her. *And Finn... what did they know about Finn?* He said little and deflected direct questions.

There was no one about when he set off down the path that took him to the other side of the village. It was no more than a mile and he had no reason to hurry, so Roger proceeded at a gentle stroll. Usually, the path was kept clear – they took turns in chopping back the brambles and moving stones that could get caught in a cart's wheels. But if someone was passing through the village and it looked too well-cared for, that would suggest a healthy and well-fed village, somewhere worth staying to rob. Such careful disarray meant he needed to pay more heed to where he was stepping.

There was a place at which the path curved away and back again to avoid the edge of the woods. A cart would need to follow it but there was no point in walking further than he needed to. He could shorten his journey by cutting through the edge of the woods.

As Roger pushed through brambles, he glanced into the depth of the woods. Something caught his eye. It was some distance away and he squinted to work out what had made the movement. *Pray God there was no wolf here.*

There'd been talk of a wolf lurking in the woods, but there was always talk of something lurking in the woods. If all the things rumoured had truly been there, there would have been no space for the trees.

But that was definitely a movement. Roger stopped and stared. Unnerved, he remained motionless, watching. *And there!* There was a beast. He could see its fur glinting among the trees. And he could smell it.

Even if it were a wolf, there might be no danger. It could be lost, abandoned by its pack because of sickness, dying of hunger like everything else. But he'd seen wolves many times and this didn't move like a wolf.

It was huge! It glided through the trees and moved with ease through the gorse and brambles. It was moving further away and had soon gone out of sight into the gorse beyond. For what seemed an eternity, Roger remained still. It didn't return and gradually he felt able to command his limbs to move. Briefly, he wondered whether to go back and do his errand later. If the beast was part of a pack, they could appear at any moment and one man couldn't battle a pack of wild beasts alone. But there was no sound, no movement, no smell – nothing to suggest danger of any sort.

However, it made sense to return to the path and take the longer route.

Roger was almost halfway when his walk was again interrupted. Momentarily surprised, he halted. Matilda was standing on the path with her back to him. Her head was bent forward, her arms bent as if she held her hands to her face. She was silent but her shoulders moved as if she were sobbing.

'Matilda?'

There was no response. Roger walked closer and hesitated. Matilda had clearly believed herself to be alone. She might not be happy to be seen in such a sorrowful state. Perhaps he should retreat and return later. Then he realised that although Matilda hadn't responded, it was likely that she had heard him and he'd feel a fool if she later asked why he hadn't stopped to help, why he'd left her alone when it was so clear she needed help. What sort of friend would he be?

So he tried again. 'Matilda?'

Nothing happened immediately, although Roger fancied Matilda's sobs had increased and her shoulders seemed to be shaking more and more unnaturally. Then, while the rest of her body remained still, her head began to slowly turn on her neck until she faced him.

Terror flooded Roger's chest. Silence thundered in his ears.

Matilda looked directly at him. Her neck was twisted backward and elongated as her head faced the wrong way. Horror and fascination fought within Roger.

Then Matilda opened her mouth to grin and he involuntarily took a step backwards, lifting his hands before him as if to ward her off. Matilda's mouth widened until Roger could see her teeth. But the smile didn't reach her eyes, which were flat and cold. Then, without turning her body, Matilda made a move towards Roger. And then another. She moved carefully and deliberately and her grin didn't waver.

Everything stopped. Roger froze to the spot in fear, unable to move any of his limbs, barely able to breathe. The world had grown very small. All that existed was in this space, this moment. There was nothing else, and he had no power over what was happening. Inside, he was screaming. She was now upon him, standing taller than man, leaning in, her face about to press into his.

Crack!

What was that? Roger blinked.

No one was standing on the path. His senses having returned, Roger gave himself a light shake as if to confirm his body was working again. Then he blinked again and stared around him, moving his head slowly to ensure he saw everything.

Nothing. There was nothing there. He was alone.

He didn't feel alone. Although he turned and walked away, forcing himself to whistle softly under his breath in an attempt to give himself some company, a part of him felt eyes watching him from a distance. A small part of him felt that a decision had been made that he was no threat and that all would be well this time.

Maerwynn watched as Roger stopped in front of Matilda's house where she was leading Thom along the path. They spoke animatedly, and then Matilda waved towards her house and Roger followed her inside. For a few minutes, Maerwynn stared at the closed door. Then she made a decision. She could visit another time.

Turning around, she walked into Kate. Maerwynn gasped in surprise and Kate giggled. 'I thought you hadn't seen me! You walk as if you're in a dream.'

Maerwynn frowned at her. 'I was thinking.' Then she realised that Kate was alone. *Odd, Kate usually had her children with her if not several other people's children as well.*

'I know what you're thinking,' said Kate. 'Where has she put her babes?'

'I wasn't,' Maerwynn lied, hoping that Kate wouldn't fill her ears with details about her children's recent actions. It was too cold to stand and endure that.

Kate leaned forward as if to impart a great secret. 'I left them with Emma's mother. Emma was there.'

Then she stood back and nodded importantly. Maerwynn had no idea what she was supposed to make of this statement. 'I need to—' she attempted, but it was too late.

Kate had launched into a long and detailed account of how her youngest, Will, had almost caught a rabbit. As it soon transpired that it wasn't actually a rabbit and that Will hadn't caught anything, Maerwynn let her thoughts wander while keeping an interested smile on her face.

'They say that Finn makes animals appear when you turn your back,' Kate concluded.

Maerwynn looked at her in confusion. 'What animals? How?'

'He says charms,' Kate said. 'Then he kills it and feasts on it. Agnes said she saw him with blood around his mouth.'

'And Agnes asked Finn and he said he had eaten an animal? Without cooking it? He'd eaten it alive? She saw this happen?'

Maerwynn's scathing tone caused Kate to flush. But it didn't silence her. 'Not Agnes. She didn't see it herself. Not the killing. But the blood must have come from somewhere. And there is the wolf.'

'What wolf?'

'In the woods. It was moving in the trees. It chased Peter away when he was looking for mushrooms. He said it was as big as an oak tree.'

Maerwynn raised her eyebrows. 'A wolf interested in mushrooms? And what has that to do with Finn?' she retorted in a contrary tone, completely bored of the conversation.

'There's always talk of a wolf being nearby when Finn appears,' Kate said obscurely.

Maerwynn opened her mouth to argue with her and then thought better of it.

'Matilda knows,' added Kate.

'Matilda knows what?'

Kate looked around as if Matilda were about to

appear. Maerwynn shivered. It really was growing cold. She needed to get back indoors before rain started to fall. 'Matilda knows what?' she repeated.

'She's always with him,' Kate said. 'He's been seen going into her house – at night.'

'I've been seen going into her house,' pointed out Maerwynn. 'And at night.'

Kate stared at her. 'You know what I mean.'

I wish I didn't, thought Maerwynn. Kate was no doubt waiting for Maerwynn to lose her temper and argue. And hoping that in temper she would reveal some new, untold information that Kate could hide away and use the next time she intercepted someone along the path. Instead, she smiled at Kate and said, 'I need to return. I need to repair my skirt – it caught on the brambles yesterday when I was looking for berries.'

Confused, Kate looked at where Maerwynn was pointing. 'That's a bad tear. It must have been a strong bush.'

Before Maerwynn could say more, there was a shout and she and Kate turned to see Peter running towards them.

'Thief!' he shouted. 'There is a thief amongst us!'

'What's happened?' asked Kate, wide-eyed.

'Come... Godfrey... ' Peter bent forward and put his hands on his knees, fighting for breath. 'I am too old for such sport,' he said, once recovered. 'Godfrey had found some apples... a tree deep in the woods... ' He wheezed. 'They were in the house and he stepped out and someone came in and took them!'

Kate clapped her hand in front of her mouth in horror. 'Another theft! And it must be someone amongst us. Who knew about the apples?'

Peter shrugged. 'Likely, many. Godfrey was drunk last night. But it can only have been within the last hour or so.'

'But hasn't someone seen anything?' asked Kate.

Peter shook his head. 'Nothing unusual.'

Maerwynn sighed. She'd have to return with Peter to comfort Agnes or she'd be accused of lacking sympathy. She patted Peter's arm and was about to suggest they went back together when a voice from behind her made her jump.

'What's happened?' asked Finn.

CHAPTER 21

November 1316

Two of Kate's children died. They hadn't eaten for three days. And no one found out for two more days because Kate sat alone with them, holding them close to her in the hope that she was wrong, that they would wake at any moment. When Maerwynn had gently pulled her away, she'd simply turned away to stare at the wall. Maerwynn touched her forehead – it was ice cold. She glanced at Roger and shook her head. Kate would soon be joining her children.

The two children who remained looked as if they would welcome death. Both hollow-eyed and pale-skinned, they huddled in the corner of the room. Maerwynn went over to them.

'You did right to come to get me,' she said gently to the girl. 'Your mama is very sick but we will care for her.'

The girl stared at her. 'The man told me to fetch you,' she said.

'The man?' Maerwynn asked, puzzled.

'I went outside and there was a man. He was watching.'

Maerwynn glanced at Roger but he shrugged. 'It wasn't me,' he said.

'Your name is Merry?' Maerwynn asked the girl.

She nodded.

'Then, Merry, will you come with me? And your brother? I have some stew I can share with you.'

Slowly, the two children stood and then the girl hesitatingly took Maerwynn's hand.

'You have food?' Roger said in amazement.

'Very little. More water than anything, but it might help. And they shouldn't stay in this house.'

'I'll take the...' Suddenly conscious of the children watching him, Roger hesitated. 'I'll take them to the church when you have gone. Kate has a cart – I can use that. But what about Kate?'

He walked over to her and grabbed her shoulders to force Kate to face him. She acquiesced but stared at him through eyes that suggested she was no longer there.

Maerwynn grimaced. 'I don't think she has long.'

With a sigh, Kate crumpled to the floor. Gently, Roger picked her up and laid her on the bed. He pulled the cover over her and she lay still.

'I'll call Matilda to sit with Kate,' Maerwynn said. 'I can call on her on the way to my house.'

'This is wrong,' said Roger as he looked at the two children who were holding tightly onto Maerwynn and staring at her wide-eyed. 'It's hard enough for us, but the children... I heard that the bishop rode to the manor only last week and they feasted. And there's talk that the monks have sealed their doors against anyone who calls for help, keeping their stores for their own use.'

'It's easy to talk,' said Maerwynn. 'And I doubt it would have been much of a feast at the manor.' Then she looked at the children. 'Go, Roger,' she said softly. 'Tell the priest there must be a funeral today.' She tugged at the children's hands and led them outside.

Matilda sat next to Kate, holding her hand. She didn't move and the only sign she was alive was her shallow, rasping breath. Matilda had tried to force ale between her lips, but to no avail. She had to restrain herself from crying out aloud when she saw it drip down Kate's chin and onto her chest.

Kate couldn't help what she did. Matilda leaned forward and whispered into her ear. 'Merry and Will are with Maerwynn. She'll care for them.' She'd told Kate this several times, but had received no reaction. This time Kate stirred slightly. Matilda stroked her hair. 'Kate?'

How could she bear it? Watching her children die while she was so helpless?

She heard the rattle deep in Kate's throat. And then Kate was a different sort of still.

Roger had been as surprised as everyone else when the new priest arrived. He'd immediately opened the doors of the church wide and announced he would say Mass every morning – and some evenings too – if the villagers wanted him to do so. The day after he arrived, he walked around the village and introduced himself to everyone he could find. Most of them looked at him in bemusement. But some of them went to Mass the next morning. And more the day following.

Father John explained that he'd come from the town and that Lady Adelaide had offered him payment to come quickly as she said the village was in sore need of counsel.

'It would have been better spent on food,' grumbled Peter.

'Some of it was,' said Father John and he gave Peter a small hard loaf from the basket by his feet.

On the third morning, Father John announced that he would say extra masses because there was an evil in the village that could only be banished by prayer. They were still hungry but at least with the new priest Kate's children would receive a proper burial.

Roger dragged the cart along the path and struggled to pull it to the church. When he flung the door open, Father John walked from the back of the church to greet him. Roger said nothing but retreated to take one body from the cart and laid it on the ground and then the other while Father John looked on in horror.

'You can't leave them here!' he said. 'They need to be laid out.'

'Someone will come,' said Roger briskly, although he

was now realising his foolishness in going straight to the church. 'How soon may they be buried?'

'This afternoon, if you wish.'

'Just before the sun goes down,' said Roger decisively. 'I'll tell everyone while you prepare.'

Before Father John could say more, Roger exited the church. He was shaking. This wasn't how things should be done. It wasn't for him to decide when Kate's children should be buried.

As he walked down the path back towards the centre of the village, a raven swooped from the skies and he had to duck to avoid it hitting his head. Then a moment later, another appeared and swooped towards Roger. To his horror, when he looked up at the sky he saw a dozen or more ravens and they flew towards him, screeching loudly. He flung his arms in front of his face and dropped to his knees.

Nothing happened.

A hand tugged at his arm. He looked up and Finn was standing next to him, looking down with an expression of concern on his face. Roger looked up at the sky and it was clear. He got to his feet and shook Finn's hand away. 'What do you want?'

'I thought you'd fallen.'

'You're always there when something goes amiss,' hissed Roger. 'You walk in the shadows and bring sorrow.'

Finn stepped back. 'I mean you no ill,' he said sincerely.

Roger walked away with determination, but he had no idea where he was walking to.

The children were buried that evening. So was Kate.

Father John had grumbled about the speed expected from him, but it was a token complaint. They needed to act together, Roger had insisted. For the last few weeks, everyone had remained in their own space, suffering the hunger in private. If they'd shared more, Kate wouldn't have been left alone in this way. Guilt lay heavily on all of them.

When Father John asked how many they expected to attend this funeral, Roger shortly said, 'Everyone.'

When he asked who would pay his fee, because it must be a higher fee than usual, considering the haste in which he needed to act, Roger glared at him.

'You can look at me in that way,' said Father John mildly, 'but payment will still be due.'

'You will receive your payment,' said Roger. 'I will pay you myself. Later.'

Father John raised his eyebrows. 'You can do this?'

Roger could not. He had no more than three pennies left. He had nothing more to sell. But the priest didn't know. What would he do when he found out? Dig them up again?

By the time the sun had begun to sink below the horizon, almost the entire village was gathered in the church.

Almost – because no one from the manor was present. Lord Robert was in town and Lady Adelaide wouldn't venture out in such terrible weather.

As they huddled around the graves in the pouring rain, thunderclaps shook their ears and every few minutes a strike of lightning illuminated their pale faces. Father John spoke as quickly as he could and the bodies were flung into the hastily dug graves with the minimum of ceremony. A little earth was shovelled on top but Father John yelled at the gravediggers that they could complete their task in the morning. The rain would only wash it away if they persisted now.

They squeezed themselves into the church. It had never been so full. There was an unspoken agreement that they would wait until the rain had lifted before they attempted to return to their homes.

'This is not natural weather,' Roger yelled at Matilda over the roar of talk. 'None of what is happening is within nature.'

'It's God's plan,' Father John said smugly.

Matilda and Roger turned to stare at him.

'God's plan?' yelled Roger. 'God planned that the skies should try to drown us, that pestilence should be amongst us and that we should starve in our beds?'

Father John stepped back. 'It is not for us to under-stand God's—'

He yelped as Roger swung a punch at him. Fortunately, Matilda grabbed his arm so his fist only grazed the priest's face.

Father John took another step back.

'What God would will this?' Roger shouted.

'He's right,' a man shouted from a few yards away. 'There's an ungodly presence amongst us.'

The chatter had completely dissolved to be replaced by an earnest muttering of agreement.

'Roger,' Matilda attempted as she pulled at his arm.

Roger ignored her. 'Someone has brought this curse to our village,' he said. 'Someone must bear the responsibility.'

'It is not of man...' Father John began. The villagers parted with their heads bowed to allow him to pass.

'Where is he?' Roger called out. 'Where is Finn? He is the stranger amongst us.'

The villagers nodded and there were calls of agreement. A few looked worried and tried to speak but were silenced by those next to them.

'No!' shouted Matilda. 'You can't blame him. The rain falls on the whole land. The pestilence and hunger is everywhere.'

Agnes pushed forward and spat in Matilda's face. In horror, Matilda looked to Roger for help but he gazed steadfastly ahead. 'Just because he warms your bed doesn't make him less evil,' said Agnes.

'He commanded the birds to attack me,' said Roger.

There was a gasp and a woman stepped forward to say, 'Since he arrived my cow gave no milk. We had to slaughter her.'

Another shouted, 'My crops rotted in the field – in one night!'

And, one by one, more shouted out about the wrongs they believed Finn had bestowed on them.

Roger reached into his tunic to pull out an old and shabby belt buckle which he held aloft. 'Cold iron! I am protected!' he yelled. 'We must act! And swiftly.'

As a cheer rang out, Matilda pushed her way through the crowd. She passed Maerwynn who was leaning against a wall.

No one stopped Matilda as she opened the church door. No one stopped her as she began her lonely walk home.

CHAPTER 22

November 1316

'Why are you here?' asked Matilda for the second time.

Father John shuffled on the stool where he sat. 'I haven't seen you at Mass,' he said. 'And people are talking.'

'They're always talking,' Matilda said dismissively. 'It quiets the rumble of their bellies.' She looked around the room. It looked bare. Anything of the slightest value had been sold long ago. Nothing remained of Galeran. 'I have no food to offer you,' she said. 'No ale to share. If that's your hope, you've come to the wrong house.'

Father John lifted a hand to silence Matilda. 'I have ample food. And the manor has sent me ale.'

Matilda looked at him closely. He carried no sack, no bundle. There was nothing in his hands, nothing by his side. 'Ample,' she said slowly.

A flush came to the priest's cheeks but he held his head high. 'It's an obligation of my position,' he said loftily, 'to maintain my health so I can care for my flock.'

'And it's an obligation of mine—' began Matilda, halting as Father John again raised his hand.

'There's an anger brewing,' he said crisply. 'They seek to uncover the wickedness that has brought the hunger and pestilence. Someone has raised their hand and caused the skies to weep so hard that it washes away the herbs. They've acted against God's will and he is angry.'

'It wasn't me,' said Matilda.

'But you may need to confess.'

Matilda was now puzzled. 'Confess to bringing the rain?'

Father John looked carefully at the ground as he spoke, avoiding looking Matilda directly in the eye. 'If that were your sin, then indeed you should confess. But that wasn't what I meant.'

Then he suddenly looked at her and the pain in his eyes made Matilda flinch.

'Someone has to be punished. Someone needs to pay. Nought will change until payment has been received.'

Matilda stood in the field, rain dripping down her face and into her mouth as she held Thom as he stood placidly. First she muttered a charm her mother had taught her. It was in Latin, the language of the church, which should give it more power, or so her mother had told her. But Matilda didn't know what a single one of the words she was saying meant – indeed, she was unsure whether she'd remembered them correctly. But if she had, it may help the plants grow.

Then she whirled around and spat to catch the devil in the eye if he were looking over her shoulder. Thom offered a whinny at her sudden movement so she patted him. And on Father John's advice she prayed to Saint Elias to stop the rainfall. And to Our Lady to protect against lightning. She'd have prayed to anything at this point in the hope that one of her prayers would work.

Just one.

Finally, she dropped to her knees and inspected the ground. A few shoots had recently emerged and she thought of leaving them so they had a chance to grow so they'd be bigger and stronger. And then of pulling them out of the ground and eating them at that moment. The thought of anything going into her mouth made it water. She pulled one from the ground. Its roots were longer than she had expected and she held it into the rain for a moment so it could wash the soil away. Then unable to wait any longer, she stuffed it into her mouth. It tasted acrid and had the texture of wool.

Sweeping her hands across the ground, Matilda uncovered more shoots and ate them as slowly as she could.

The rain was falling so heavily that Matilda didn't encounter anyone as she walked slowly home. She tied Thom up and then decided to call on Roger. She hadn't seen him for several days now and was worried that he was sick. It wasn't good how things had been left. And surely people would be calmer now and she could sow seeds of sense amongst them.

In fact, she hadn't seen anyone but Maerwynn. No one had knocked on her door. When she'd been out, people had muttered that they were busy or hurried and had turned away from her. When she'd knocked on Agnes's door, Agnes had stared at her silently and closed the door again without uttering a word.

Matilda had thought that people would have calmed by now. She had been wrong.

Other doors hadn't opened at all.

Maerwynn had called briefly the day before saying that she was going to the manor as Lady Adelaide was sick again and couldn't stay long but she'd return soon. And she'd handed Matilda a small heel of bread and a sliver of cheese. Matilda's demurring was only a token effort.

Roger hesitated when he saw Matilda at his door but she held her head high and simply stared at him. He turned aside and motioned her to step inside.

'Sit by the fire,' he said. 'You're wet through.'

Gratefully, Matilda huddled in front of the fire. She'd had no wood for a few days now and it was too wet to gather any. Roger sat on a stool nearby and looked anxiously at the door.

'Are you well?' he said to Matilda.

'As well as anyone, but no one wishes to speak with me,' said Matilda bluntly. 'Even you it seems.'

Roger winced. 'I'm sorry, Matilda. I had so much to take care of.' Then he fell silent.

'What have you needed to take care of?' Matilda asked curiously.

Before he could answer, a loud knock at the door made her jump. Roger opened the door and Howard entered, shaking the rain from his hair. He nodded to Matilda as he entered and then immediately launched into a barrage of words aimed at Roger. 'I spoke with Lord Robert,' he began. 'He agreed and has sent a man to ride into town to get a magistrate. He should return before nightfall and then we—'

'Why do you need a magistrate?' asked Matilda.

Howard looked at her as if she'd grown another head. 'It is a matter of law,' he said. 'We can't simply place a sentence on someone outside the law. That way lies madness.'

A trickle of fear travelled down Matilda's back. 'What sentence?' She stood up and walked over to Howard. 'What sentence?' she said again.

'Matilda…' Roger looked at her sheepishly.

As if he hadn't spoken, Howard continued. 'Finn must be punished for what he has done.'

'But what has he done?' asked Matilda in a quiet voice.

'He must be punished,' said Howard decisively.

'Then why not now?' demanded Roger. 'We could send some men out to find him now. There is no need to wait for the magistrate!'

'We will need to find him...' Howard said.

Matilda looked at Roger and then at Howard while considering her words. 'And what happens after you find him?'

Walking back home Matilda felt as if she was being followed, but every time she turned there was nothing there.

Or almost nothing.

In the corner of her eye, she could see a blurred shape, low on the ground, like a large dog. But no matter how quickly she twisted and turned, it remained at the periphery of her vision.

It was already growing dark and Matilda decided to climb into bed fully dressed and wait for - hopefully - a better morning. She curled up tightly and shivered. The cold felt worse for her having spent some time in front of Roger's fire.

Sleep would not come.

Matilda curled up more tightly and allowed her mind to wander. She thought back to days of sunlight and plenty. She remembered Galeran's laughter and the first days she had Thom. She thought of hope and what might have been.

And she wept.

A knock at the window startled her. Matilda listened and there it was again. And a soft voice called her name. Slowly, she emerged from her bed and listened again. Someone was definitely calling her name. She opened the door to find Finn there.

Matilda offered him a smile and he walked inside. 'I haven't seen you for days and days,' she said.

'I went—' said Finn, hesitating, '—to see if I could find any food.'

'To town?'

Finn ignored Matilda's question. 'Have you been well?' he asked.

'Well enough,' said Matilda. 'But people are acting oddly.'

'People...'

'Did you find any food?' Matilda's heart lifted. In the dark she couldn't see Finn that clearly. Perhaps he was carrying something.

'Some. A little. I have some beans and two eggs.'

'Oh!' So much more than Matilda had hoped. So much more.

'If you light the fire, we can make a meal,' he said.

Matilda's heart fell. 'I have no firewood. Nothing to burn. It has been too wet to gather wood.'

'Sit.'

Confused, Matilda sat next to the fire. Behind her, Finn made a few shuffling noises and then tossed his tunic onto the fire. She gasped as he pulled out a flint to set it alight.

'You cannot do this! The cold...'

'Don't fret,' said Finn crisply. 'I'll wear another. This one is dry as it was under it.'

Within a few minutes the tunic was burning and Matilda cooked the eggs in a pan and they ate them while waiting for the beans to boil. There were no herbs to add to the beans so they would taste dull, but – *beans*!

Then they talked for hours. Matilda told Finn about what had happened in the village since she'd last seen him. He shook his head sadly. And as the sun was rising, Finn told her a story of a dog he had met while walking the road to town and how it had followed him from the moment he encountered it. 'A sad looking thing,' he said. 'His owner must have died because he seemed so lost.'

'Is he with you now?'

'He stayed with me for three days and one morning he wasn't by my side. I think someone must have stolen him.' Finn moved closer to Matilda. 'People are eating—'

Matilda clapped her hand to her mouth in horror. 'Eating dogs?' But despite herself, she salivated at the thought.

And then to make her smile, Finn told her a tale:

One day there arrived in a village a dog that was made of many colours. From one side, he appeared to be black and white. From another, he looked bright red. He wore a golden chain with a bell around his neck. When the bell rang, anyone who heard it would forget their sorrows.

It brought many people good comfort. And when

people's hearts grew light they passed it around their village so all might feel well. And when the whole village was filled with laughter and love, the blacksmith said he would take the dog to the next village so they too could be happy.

But in the next village there was a woman whose husband had gone to war. Nothing had been heard of him for many years, but still she waited for his return. The dog ran from house to house, his bell jangling and soon he was met with smiles wherever he went.

But the woman would not be truly happy because she knew her husband, her true love, would not be happy without her. So she took the bell off the chain. She would not tell anyone where she'd hidden it and in time, new sorrows beset the village. The dog still offered comfort where he could, but that wasn't enough.

So the villagers decided they should kill the dog because his purpose had changed. And they argued and argued whether this should be so, and all the time the woman thought of her husband and the hidden bell.

Finn paused.

'Did they kill the dog?' Matilda asked in fascination.

'That is another tale and I will tell it to you another time.' Finn stood. 'It's becoming light. Agnes will be rising soon so I can return and tell her that I'll need a bed there again.'

'No!' said Matilda leaping to her feet and grabbing Finn's arm. 'You mustn't!'

'Why?' asked Finn in a puzzled tone.

'They're seeking you because... I did tell you! They believe that someone has cast an evil charm on the village. They believe that must be you!'

Finn laughed. 'Maybe one or two people think in that way, but the others will know that hunger and sickness is everywhere. I don't have such powers!' He laughed again.

'You don't understand,' said Matilda in frustration. 'The magistrate is in the village. He has the power to—'

'A learned man has the intelligence to tell people I have not done such a thing,' insisted Finn.

'But he won't if he's paid well enough. And if he does, every time you walk alone you'll need to watch behind you as well as ahead of you.'

'I'll be safe.'

'You won't. You must leave.'

'You wish me to leave?' Finn asked softly.

'Yes! No!'

'Then I shall and I shall not,' said Finn, gravely.

Matilda smiled weakly. 'I don't want you to leave, but you must leave.' It had taken so much of her strength to say this. More than anything, she wanted Finn to remain by her side. 'It's not safe,' she added.

'I understand.' Finn leaned forward and briefly kissed Matilda. Her heart swelled at the touch, she realised all of a sudden as she drew back and looked into his eyes that all this time they had been falling in love with each other. This is what true love felt like and she never wanted to be without it; without him. She leaned into his embrace and kissed him deeply again.

'I'll leave but there will be a time for me to return. Be patient.'

And before Matilda could say anything more, he had gone.

CHAPTER 23

November 1316

Howard and the men from the manor searched every house in the village for a sign of Finn. In Matilda's case, that involved casting an eye around the room and briefly looking in the bed. There was nowhere that Finn could have hidden. Nonetheless, Howard promised Matilda dire consequences should she have harboured him. She slammed the door loudly as he departed.

Then she sat silently on the stool and waited for them to return. For they would return, she had no doubt of that.

Roger rubbed his back and then his knee. He felt as if he were a hundred years old. Every part of his body ached and he had to keep blinking to keep his vision clear. And there was a ringing in his ears that wouldn't go no matter what he did.

'Roger!'

He turned to look at Howard. 'No trace of him,' he

said crisply. This was the second time they'd combed the woods and all they'd found so far was a very surprised squirrel. 'Wherever he is, it isn't in the woods. Unless he's dug a hole and buried himself in it.'

'Do you think he could have done that?' asked Howard.

Roger stared at him. 'Of course not. It was a joke.'

Howard reddened. 'He has to be somewhere. Someone must know – or be hiding him. We have to keep searching.'

Roger made a decision. 'This is a waste of time,' he said. 'There's nowhere left to search. We will have to tell the magistrate there's no reason for him to wait. I'm going back. I'll speak to him if you want.' He turned to walk away.

Howard grabbed his arm and spun him around to face him. Roger felt the world spin and bile rise in his throat. It sounded as if Howard was speaking from a long way away. He struggled to make sense of his words.

'You may be sweet on her,' said Howard, 'But if she's been protecting him she will have to be punished. You must understand that.'

'What are you talking about?'

Howard looked very strange. He was fading and his voice sounded very small. His mouth was still moving but now no sound came from it. And he'd almost faded away. *Was he still there?* Roger hit out in the general direction of where he'd last seen Howard and heard a yelp. He hit out again but this time there was nothing.

And the trees. They swayed and were whispering at him. *They were laughing at him!*

A bird swooped from above towards Roger and he screamed in terror. Unidentified voices were shouting his name, dozens of them, calling him again and again. *Roger... Roger... Roger...*

His head hurt. It hurt so much. He'd had enough.

Roger sighed and slumped to the ground.

Maerwynn tutted to herself. *How quickly do they think I can move?* 'I'm coming,' she yelled. She hastily put her tunic on and smoothed her hair under her cap. Granted, it was late to be sleeping but she was always so tired nowadays.

She flung the door open to find Howard lifting his fist to beat on it again. 'You must come,' he said. 'Roger is sick – very sick. You have herbs to give him? Something curative?'

'What sort of sick?' Maerwynn asked as she turned back into the house and opened the box in which she kept her herbs. Her efforts to become invaluable to the people of the village and more importantly the manor had its drawbacks she thought.

'I don't know. He fell to the ground. And now he raves. He seems to have lost his senses.'

Maerwynn held up her hand to stem the flow of words as she rummaged through her box. 'When did this happen?'

'No more than a few moments ago. I came right away. Can you heal him? Can—'

Howard fell silent. Maerwynn turned to see what had claimed his attention. He was staring at the table. 'You have white bread?'

Maerwynn stood and watched him in silence. Howard walked up to the table and inspected it more closely. 'You have white bread. Like the white bread from the manor. And—' He reached to the table and Maerwynn put her hands in front of her face. 'Chicken bones,' Howard said flatly. 'But you've never kept chickens. Joan said that you reeked dishonesty. She told everyone that she'd heard you'd been forced from your home before arriving here. That you'd been disgraced after you'd stolen from an old woman under your care. We thought it was no more than another of her tales. But even a teller of tales will sometimes tell a true one.' Then he shook his head. 'We won't speak of this now. There isn't time.'

He stared at Maerwynn but she'd frozen and was unable to speak. It hadn't been her fault. There are things that medicine can't cure. The old woman would have died anyway – and she wouldn't have begrudged Maerwynn her trifles, especially after the hours Maerwynn had spent clucking at her and holding her hand. Not that her sons had seen it that way. She'd lived in that village all her life and they'd flung her out without a coin to her name. It had been a hard journey to her current home. She preferred to forget what she'd had to do to survive along the way.

Maerwynn had felt like fleeing there and then as she had done before. But under Howard's presence she had to go with him or she may not make it out of the village at all. Besides, she liked it here and didn't want to leave. *Perhaps she could convince Howard in some way to keep her secret. A person like he could always be bought somehow,* she thought to herself while gathering her things. 'This is such a small matter,' she chimed, attempting to be as demure as she could. 'I can offer you a share in my ... well, *anything* I can. A man of your standing could demand anything of me,' she continued.

'I am not interested in anything *you* have to offer,' he said in disgust; knowing full well what she was trying to do and what her 'offer' was.

The seconds felt like minutes to her. Each slowly giving way to the next.

'Come, we need to aid Roger,' Howard said briskly as he walked towards the door.

Relieved by the change of subject and suspicious that the fattest, most manipulative man in the area was more concerned with a peasant's health than anything else, Maerwynn snatched up a bundle of herbs and silently followed him.

Roger was curled tightly into a ball where Howard had left him. Maerwynn shook her head as she dropped to her knees and looked at him closely. Although Roger kept his eyes tightly closed, he was obviously aware of their presence as he whimpered.

'Roger?' Maerwynn said gently.

He opened one eye and gasped. Maerwynn got back to her feet. 'Help him up,' she said briskly to Howard. 'We need to get him home.'

Without uttering a word, Howard pulled Roger to his feet. Roger didn't resist and with a combination of coaxing and pulling, Howard and Maerwynn slowly persuaded him to walk home. He muttered as they walked along but nothing he said made sense. Once they reached his house, Roger shrugged himself free of their grasp and tumbled onto his bed with a sigh.

'What's wrong with him?' asked Howard.

Maerwynn shook her head. 'I'm not sure but I think...' At that moment she noticed a small basket of mushrooms on the table. She picked them up saying, 'It's probably best if I destroy these. Roger will be well after a sleep. I'll stay with him.'

Relieved that it was no longer his problem, Howard nodded and turned to leave. Then he hesitated and said, 'I needn't say anything about earlier. You can repay that debt later.'

It took them longer to come for Matilda than she'd expected. She'd thought of running, but that would be like admitting guilt. She'd thought of hiding, but that seemed cowardly. And where would she go, where would she hide with no money and no one to turn to.

She'd hoped that Finn would return before they came. But he hadn't, and when they came and said that the magistrate wanted to question her, she nodded and picked up her shawl, wrapping it around herself closely. As they walked to the manor, faces peered from doors, immediately retreating when Matilda returned their looks.

The magistrate was a thin man with a long pointed nose and greying hair. He was dressed in good clothes that looked as if he was at least their third owner. And he looked as if he would have preferred to have been anywhere other than where he was. Matilda sat on a stool opposite the table where the magistrate sat with Robert on one side and Father John on the other. Howard hovered behind them.

'It doesn't matter how many times you ask me,' said Matilda in frustration. 'I don't know where he is.'

'Would you tell us if you did?' asked the magistrate.

She held his gaze defiantly. 'No,' she said softly. 'What crime has he committed?'

The magistrate glanced at Lord Robert who nodded. 'We don't yet know,' he said carefully. 'But he arrived with the hunger. Pestilence, murder and theft followed him closely. It would be well to investigate this matter.'

'He stands accused of commanding the birds of the air,' interrupted Father John.

'Not by me,' said the magistrate briskly, shutting down 'fairy John' as he privately referred to him.

'And of causing a field of wheat to rot in an hour,' added Father John.

'I would like to know how he did such a thing,' said Matilda calmly.

The magistrate looked pained and leaned over to whisper in Robert's ear. In turn, Robert nodded and beckoned Howard and muttered something at him.

Howard nodded. 'Father John,' he said, 'would you be so kind as to attend to Lady Adelaide? It has been many days since her last confession and she sorely needs counsel.'

Father John looked doubtful but Howard walked to the door and pointedly held it open. With a sigh, he got to his feet and allowed himself to be escorted from the room.

Matilda clamped a hand onto her mouth to hide her involuntary smile. But she was too late.

'This isn't a laughing matter,' said the magistrate. 'There have been many thefts, and murders of the most gruesome sort. Those haven't been done by "birds of the air".'

'Why do you believe Finn to be responsible? I suppose Finn was responsible for Martin's death, when he fell from Giant's Grave Hill? For all the deaths there have been here? Edward was mauled like meat months before Finn arrived. Roger can attest to this.' Her temper and tone now rising.

'I don't know who's responsible,' the magistrate said. 'I ask questions so that I might discover that. I need to ask him questions.'

'Can a man command the weather, the air or ground? Can he be in two places at the same time? This is madness!' said Matilda. 'He told me of a beast that lurks, and others have said the same. Something that would make even Lord Robert cry for his mother like a babe.' She cast a scornful glance to the Lord.

'You would say that and perhaps he did too. You're only trying to move blame, with no real proof.' The magistrate dismissed her claim like an echo of Audri's trial. 'I have—' The magistrate indicated a piece of paper. 'I have testimony here from many villagers. They say you have consorted with this man. That you have taken him into your bed and that you have covered for his crimes. They say you have aided him with witchcraft and that you have killed for the sake of jealousy. They say—'

Matilda glared at the magistrate dumbfounded and glanced at Robert, noticing his smirk.

'This is what they say. And such testimony needs to be assessed. When the whole village speaks against someone …'

'The whole village?'

The magistrate looked at Robert. 'All who were asked,' said Robert. 'And many who weren't. Too many to ignore.'

'But there must be those who vouch for me!' said Matilda. 'I've spent my whole life in this village. They've known me since I was a babe. I am no witch. Have you spoken with Roger?'

'Roger can't speak for anyone,' said Robert. 'He has taken leave of his senses.'

'And you believe this man?' She hissed at the judge pointing a finger at Robert. 'I know what kind of a man he is, I heard he and Howard talk of murder when I worked for Lady Adelaide.'

'Enough.' The justice commanded.

When they realised that Matilda wasn't going to tell them what they wanted to hear, no matter what they said, Robert called one of his men and she was locked in a room while they considered what to do next. As she passed, Lord Robert leaned in and with a squeeze of her arm said 'I will keep you company tonight.'

CHAPTER 24

November 1316

A few minutes after the key had turned, the door opened again and the man offered Matilda a platter with bread and cheese on it and a goblet of ale. She looked at him in amazement.

'It isn't much,' he said, 'but you will be of no use if you're too hungry to speak, and the magistrate commanded it.'

Matilda devoured it within seconds and groaned as her belly objected. But it was a good objection.

Then she waited. Locked in there with her thoughts of Finn and how they should have left when they had the chance. She couldn't help but think of Audri all those months ago in a place like this. Knowing you're damned here, in this cold dank pit with no light to guide you to hope.

She waited for Lord Robert and his men, knowing he is a man of his word and this was the perfect opportunity for him to finish what he'd started a few weeks ago.

Eventually the door creaked open and Matilda got to her feet. To her amazement, Adelaide entered with her finger to her lips, accompanied by a man with a long white beard.

'Why are you here?' Matilda implored.

'Well, not to ask you to finish my needlework while I read,' Adelaide smiled. 'Master Edmund would speak with you,' she said so quietly that Matilda could barely hear her.

Edmund nodded and drew close to Matilda. 'You will wear her ladyship's cloak and leave with me,' he said. 'They won't question us if you remain hooded. Don't speak. Don't look at anyone, but don't look away either. If you look too much at the ground, they'll ask questions. Raise your nose to the sky as if they're too unimportant for your attention. Can you do that?'

Matilda nodded.

'We must leave now,' Edmund said. 'They believe you're hiding the stranger. And they believe you to be a witch.'

Adelaide slid her cloak from her shoulders and passed it to Matilda.

'Then you must die or disappear,' said Edmund.

'I don't understand,' said Matilda. 'They spoke of witchcraft but it didn't seem that the magistrate believed such a slur. What has happened?'

Adelaide glanced at Edmund before saying, 'Maerwynn has told Howard that she has witnessed you consorting with the devil.'

Matilda stepped back and clapped her hand to her mouth in horror. 'Maerwynn? There must be a mistake. Why should she say such a thing?'

'I don't know,' said Edmund. He pulled the hood forward to hide Matilda's face. 'You don't have time to worry about this. I will lead you to the church and you can wait there until dark. It should be safe as Father John will be spending the night at the manor.'

'But what do I do then?' asked Matilda.

'This is as much as we can do for you,' said Edmund.

'And why do you help me?'

Edmund shrugged. 'I don't know.' He looked directly at Adelaide, who smiled.

'Because Finn awaits you,' she said. 'If there was a man who would make me happy and you could give me that, would you not do so?'

Matilda could do nothing but smile at the new hope she'd been given.

'The fool,' Adelaide said in an affectionate tone. 'He would be long gone by now if his senses were still with him.'

'Wait!' Matilda cried urgently, more loudly than she'd intended. A silence gripped them all for a moment as they waited for the sound of footsteps to discover them. 'They will know I have gone.' She grabbed Lady Adelaide by the arm. 'The Lord, your husband, she said he would come tonight.' she whispered in desperation. Her eyes fell to the floor 'I…' Matilda choked.

'Then we must make haste.'

Matilda was curled up tightly in the corner of the church behind a pile of wood. Edmund had placed it there before he left her. 'If someone merely glances into the church, they won't notice you,' he said. 'And if they search the church, you'll see them before they see you. They will assume you are running under cover of night. Wait until morning before you move.'

'And where do I go?'

'Lady Adelaide said you must wait,' persisted Edmund.

So Matilda waited.

It was almost light when Finn arrived. She yelped and he put a finger to his lips. 'Come,' he said quietly. Matilda scrambled to her feet unsteadily, stiff after being hunched up for so many hours. Finn led her out of the church and into the woods.

'They'll search for me,' Matilda whispered nervously.

'They will. We don't have much time.'

Matilda looked around. The wood was beginning to awaken and a songbird trilled on a nearby tree.

'And if they find you, they will take you to trial and kill you as a witch,' Finn added. 'So it would be better if they found you dead.'

Matilda stepped away from him. She stared at Finn. He held no weapon but he was much bigger than her and—

Finn laughed. 'There are many ways of dying. Will you trust me?'

She nodded. 'I have always trusted you.'

'When I leave you, go deeper into the woods.' Finn pointed. 'You'll find a hollow in a tree twenty yards in that direction. Enter it and pull leaves around you. And wait for my return.'

Finn's face took on a strange expression and he murmured and swayed. His body shimmered and waved and it was hard for Matilda to look directly at him. Then his face began to melt and to take on a new shape. He was hard to look at. Briefly, Matilda closed her eyes and when she reopened them, she saw herself staring back at her.

She stepped back in horror. Finn held his hands out beseechingly. 'Do not fear, it's still me,' he said in his usual voice.

'What have you done?' cried Matilda in amazement.

'It is what I am,' said Finn.

Matilda extended a hand and touched him. 'Is this an illusion?'

'Of sorts,' said Finn. Unexpectedly, he grinned widely. 'It will be different if they find *me* dead. I can smell Lord Robert's dogs have been on your trail for a while now. Go hide. I will return.'

Everything altogether began to make some kind of wonderful sense to her. And before Matilda could say more, he gathered up his skirts and ran from the woods.

Finn ran. Faster than he'd ever run before. But he wouldn't outrun men, horses and dogs, and this was his trick. It was only a matter of time – a very short time – until they caught up with him. He could make that time shorter. Still running, Finn slowed a little, but still springing forward with ease, up the steep embankment of the Giant's Grave Hill. Enough to close the gap between him and his pursuers.

He reached the top and glanced behind him. Their shouts and the thundering sounds of hooves on the ground grew louder. The dogs yapped intensely. They were almost upon him. Finn smiled. Turning his back to the riders, he glanced at the crevice below. He looked back at the riders again, allowing them to speed a little closer. He spread his arms and flung himself down. Here he lay still, eyes glazed open, an unnatural bend in his neck and face bloodied.

The twelve men who'd been in pursuit of him halted their horses at the top of the crevice and looked down.

'There will be no trial,' said Lord Robert. 'She can't have survived that. A pity, I had promised her to some of my men,' he mused to Howard. 'You'll have to find another whore to warm your beds tonight,' he called to those listening.

'Find a way down, and take some rope, you'll have to go on foot. Take the body to the church and call Maerwynn to lay it out,' Howard ordered.

The two men turned their horses and rode leisurely back to the manor.

The church smelt musty and of sadness. Howard led Maerwynn inside and pointed to the far end. 'Make haste,' he said. 'If others find she is here there will be calls against keeping something so ungodly on sacred ground.'

'Why here?' asked Maerwynn.

Howard prodded Matilda's corpse with his foot. 'She isn't ungodly, only foolish.'

'But Father John—'

'And he is a bigger fool. Make haste.'

Howard turned to leave and Maerwynn called at his back, 'My debt to you is done.'

He froze and then slowly turned to face her. 'You have nought to fear from me,' he said. 'Your sins are yours to own. I have better things to do than join the tongue-waggers.' A cruel smile of indifference worked its way along his face.

Maerwynn nodded. She wasn't sure if she trusted him but what more could she do? Howard stared at her for a moment longer and then shrugged and left the church.

Maerwynn dropped to her knees and turned the body so she could see Matilda's face. She closed Matilda's eyes and stroked her cheek gently, gasping as an eye opened and winked.

Matilda jumped to her feet, rounded on Maerwynn

and slowly stepped backwards. As Maerwynn watched, the corpse shimmered and shook and became as bright as the sun. She turned away for a moment and then looked back to see Finn standing before her.

'I knew you were a strange one,' hissed Maerwynn.

'And I knew you weren't to be trusted,' said Finn. 'There must be a burial today.'

Maerwynn nodded. 'I understand.'

'I'd warrant you have more than one debt to repay,' Finn said gravely.

Maerwynn took a step away from Finn and held out her hands in supplication.

Finn smiled. 'You can't pay what you owe Matilda to me. There are no pleas that will do that.'

'You think—'

'You know nothing about how I think,' said Finn. 'And it isn't important. But if you feel your soul has grown darker, if you have betrayed a trust, you need to release yourself from your burden. I cannot do it for you, nor can Howard, or anyone else.'

Father John hiccoughed and swayed on his feet. He stank of wine. 'Shouldn't we wait for the magistrate's judgement?' he asked in a puzzled tone.

Finn lay prone on the floor, wrapped in a winding sheet.

'She can't be buried on consecrated ground,' insisted Father John.

217

'She won't be,' said Maerwynn, adding gently, 'I understand that this must bring you pain. Why don't you go and rest? I'll find help and this can be completed before you awaken.'

'But you can't dig a grave and bury a body alone.'

Maerwynn laughed. 'I don't intend to try.' She leaned forward and patted Father John's arm. 'You needn't worry. Send for Roger. He'll help me.'

Father John yawned widely and shrugged. 'Make sure the body is gone before I return.'

Roger was rubbing his eyes and looking distinctly pale when he arrived at the church. He was carrying a spade. 'The priest sent a boy to get me,' he said. 'He said you need me to help bury Matilda. Is she here?' He looked around in confusion and rubbed his eyes again. 'What's happened? I've been so sick, I feel that I have lost years.'

Maerwynn cooed 'All is well, you are alone? Are you certain you're alone?

'Of course I'm alone,' said Roger tetchily.

'We must bury Matilda in the woods,' said Maerwynn.

'Without a priest? Alone? Now?'

When Maerwynn didn't answer, Roger picked up the bundle from the floor and flung it over his shoulder. 'Heavier than I'd have thought,' he mumbled. He staggered but soon regained his balance and left the church, Maerwynn close behind him helping him with the weight of the body and carrying the spades.

Fortunately, no one else was to be seen as they entered the woods, but Maerwynn wanted to take no risks and urged Roger to move further, faster. Roger huffed and puffed but didn't protest. Finally, she said, 'Here. This is good enough.'

Roger laid his bundle on the ground and inspected the area. They were in a small clearing and the bare ground held no more than a few twigs and some sparse grass.

'Dig a hole,' said Maerwynn. 'A deep hole.'

'I know what a grave looks like,' said Roger testily. He stuck the bottom of his spade into the ground and turned over the soil. 'This is wrong,' he added. 'This is not how you bury someone. This is not good enough for Matilda.' But he continued to dig, intermittently wiping trickling tears from his muddied face.

'Poor Roger,' said Maerwynn sympathetically. 'Your senses aren't returned yet, are they?'

'It feels as if there's a man beating a hammer inside my head,' Roger said in a weakened voice. A sudden strength overtook him and he began to dig faster and more determinedly.

'I will return shortly,' Maerwynn said suddenly.

Roger shook his head as if to clear it from cobwebs and continued to turn over the earth.

It didn't take Maerwynn long to reach Matilda's house and the moment Thom saw her, he whinnied in recognition. 'Good boy,' she said briskly and whispered a charm in his ear Finn had told her to use in case he was not willing to go with her. No one would think twice about her taking Thom. Someone needed to care for him and she would be relieving them of a task.

The few people Maerwynn saw as she rode back towards the woods averted their gaze. But it was likely sorrow that Maerwynn had been drawn to associate with a witch rather than a belief that she had committed any sin. It could be resolved later. She would find the right lies to suffice their questions; and they would soon come.

She had to dismount and coax Thom into the woods. When they arrived in the clearing he gave a delighted whinny and tried to snuffle at the bundle on the ground. Maerwynn clucked at him and held him fast. 'That looks deep enough,' she said to Roger.

Roger nodded and rubbed his back before turning to pick up the bundle in the winding sheet.

'No,' said Maerwynn. She dropped to her knees and began to unwrap the winding sheet.

Roger stared, dumbfounded as Finn emerged. 'Where is Matilda?' he pleaded in anguish and disbelief.

'Safe,' said Finn yawning widely.

'Go,' said Maerwynn. She grabbed the sheet and flung it into the hole. Finn smiled as he walked over to Thom who nuzzled him.

'I don't understand,' said Roger as they watched Finn and Thom walk away. 'Am I dreaming, still?'

Maerwynn laughed. 'I'll explain later. Now we must fill in the hole.'

Roger shook his head and did as she said, too deflated by the emotions and sickness of the past few days to object.

Matilda had fallen asleep. She awakened as the leaves and branches she had arranged around herself were pulled away. Blinking furiously, she saw Finn's face. Her heart swelled with the sight of him and she couldn't hide her happiness.

'Is it done?' she asked, pulling him towards her in an embrace.

'It is done, Roger and Maerwynn are still in the woods, do you want to speak with them before we leave? You may never see them again,' said Finn.

'You could have left long ago.'

Finn smiled. 'Not without you.'

Matilda paused for some moments before finally speaking. 'You endangered yourself to stay with me, I won't allow us to be in danger any longer. I will not see them, there is nothing more to say.'

Finn pulled Matilda from the hollow and smoothed leaves from her hair. 'Where do you wish to go?'

'We will find out together,' said Matilda. She took his hand and they walked through the wood. Thom was tied to a nearby tree and Matilda exhaled with relief when she saw him. Finn lifted Matilda onto Thom's back. They walked calmly into the deep wood.

Epilogue

Maerwynn was deep in thought as she sat on the church step. A movement caught her attention. She held her breath and squinted. There, between the trees, was the shape of a beast, walking slowly and regally, as if it owned the woods.

Slowly, Maerwynn got to her feet and took two steps towards it. She stopped as the shape also halted.

She waited.

The wolf came into view. Her silver-white fur was thick and glossy and she walked lightly on her powerful feet. The wolf padded across the churchyard towards the village looming over the broken walls that lined the path. Maerwynn followed her.

Ahead of them was Father John deep in conversation with Peter and Agnes. The wolf approached. The rogue now unafraid of the prey she'd been hunting. They stepped out of her path and she strolled onwards.

'There is your death-bringer,' shouted Maerwynn

when she reached them. The wolf halted and sniffed the air.

'A beast doesn't remove the sins of man,' said Father John.

'He was a thief,' burst out Agnes. 'And he colluded with your witch-friend.'

Suddenly, the wolf turned and looked directly into Maerwynn's eyes.

'I see you,' said Maerwynn softly. 'We all see you now.'

The wolf howled and Maerwynn began to weep.

Printed in Great Britain
by Amazon

78194401R00133